North Queensland in Black and White

A social history
with views, stories and archaeology

Indigenous people are warned that this book contains names and images of people who have died.

North Queensland in Black and White

A social history
with views, stories and archaeology

Patsy Coverdale

CATTAC PRESS

Published by CATTAC PRESS
17 Casella Street Mitcham Vic 3132 Australia. www.cattac.com.au.
© Copyright Patricia Dawn Coverdale 2016.
First published 2011.

Apart from any use as permitted under the Copyright Act 1968, no part may be reproduced by any process without prior written permission from the copyright holder. Every attempt has been made to trace and obtain copyright. Should any copyright not be acknowledged, please contact CATTAC PRESS.

Photographers: Patsy Coverdale and others.
The cover photographs are referred to on pages viii, 4, 58, 60, 161 and 195.
Editor: Amanda Coverdale.
Designer, subeditor and cartographer: Garth Coverdale.
Cover designer: Elise Wade.
Printer and distributor: Ingram.
Bookseller: Your favourite bookshop.
Typeset in Garamond Premier Pro 12/14.4.

National Library of Australia Cataloguing-in-Publication entry
Creator: Coverdale, Patsy, author.

Title: North Queensland in black and white: a social history with stories, views and archaeology / Patsy Coverdale.

Edition: 2nd edition

ISBN: 9780994585707 (paperback)

Notes: Includes bibliographical references.

Subjects: Bama (Australian people)—Queensland—Cairns Region
 —Race relations—History.
Bama (Australian people)—Queensland—Cairns Region—History.
Bama (Australian people) —Queensland—Cairns Region—Antiquities.
Bama (Australian people) —Queensland—Cairns Region
 —Government relations—History.
Bama (Australian people) —Queensland—Cairns Region
 —Social conditions—History.
Pioneers—Queensland—Cairns Region—History.
Cairns Region (Qld.) —Race relations—History.
Cairns Region (Qld.) —Emigration and immigration—History.

Dewey Number: 305.89915099436

CONTENTS

	A Thank You Note	vii
	Introduction	1
	Words used in North Queensland	6
	List of Illustrations	9
	Maps	11
1	Home on the Mountain	15
2	The Romance Between Cultures	25
3	The Urban Jungle	31
4	Keeping Records	35
5	Mona Mona and Yarrabah Missions	55
6	Steven and Mona Fagan	61
7	The Mission Years	65
8	Self-Destruction	69
9	Takeaway Children	79
10	Medicine Men	83
11	Captured in Pictures	89
12	Finding a Voice	101
13	Civilisation and Violence	109
14	What's in a Name	111
15	The Power of Myths	119
16	The Bama Way of Life	127
17	Women's Business	133
18	Men's Business	139
19	The First People	143
20	Looking after the Country	149
21	A Living Archaeology	157
22	Secrets in the Stone	163
23	Bush Foods and Tools	167
24	Changing Land and Seas	171
25	Conclusion	177

References		179
Appendix 1	J. Birdsell on the Bama survey	188
Appendix 2	F. A. Hagenauer on Wujal Wujal	190
Appendix 3	T. Bottoms, I. A. Staff and C. P. Ahern on plant toxins	192
Appendix 4	E. Mjoberg on cannibals	193
Appendix 5	P. D. Coverdale on six fingers	194
	About the Author	196

A THANK YOU NOTE

Some memorials are not in the place where you expect to find them. I want to thank the Murris who have befriended and trusted me with their stories: they include members of the Djabugay clans and other Bama tribes, members of the Aboriginal and Torres Strait Island Council, Steven and Mona Fagan, Muriel and Phillip Oui, their daughter Pamela, Mercy Baird of the Cape York Land Council office, Torres Strait Island Councillors when I was young, lawyer Noel Pearson, magistrate Pat O' Shane, and Patrick and Shirley O' Shane.

I am most grateful for the help and hospitality of Ailsa Tenni, Kelvin Hill and his widow Helen, Marie Copeman of Freshwater, Dr Christopher Anderson, Dr Colin and Carlyn Mathews, Ron Edwards and staff of the Department of Natural Resources and the Environment, Victoria.

I offer my acknowledgments and thanks to the Cairns Historical Society and Museum and their secretary Gil Jennex, Professor Peter Sutton (anthropologist) and Kate Alport (archives access officer) of the South Australian Museum, Cairns historian Dr Timothy Bottoms, George Skeene, Douglas Seaton, Mick Miller, Sir David Attenborough, linguist Dr R. W. Dixon, translator Siwi Fryer, Dr Ian Ring, Dr Beverly Raphael, Dr Richard Trahair, Dr N. Kowalenko, Dr P. Kershaw, Dr M. Bullen, J. Loney, Dr H. Brayshaw, Dr M. Dodson, Dr P. Dodson, Dr W. Gilbert, Dr J. Morton, Dr T. Lowe, Dr A. Thorne, J. Altmann, R. Gilroy, Janice Kamrin, and archaeologists Dr Bruno David, Dr S. Holdaway, Dr Richard Cosgrove, Dr N. Horsfall, Dr I. Hodder, Dr N. Peterson, Dr I. McBryde, Dr J. Allen, Dr M. J. Morwood and Dr D. R. Hobbs, Dr C. Gosden and Dr C. Pavlides, Dr D. E. Yen and Ewen McPhee.

NQ in Black and White

Other authors I consulted include Dr Joseph Birdsell, Dr G. Cowlishaw, Dr G. Bolton, Dr G. A. Wood, Prof B. Smith, Dr Henry Reynolds, Dr Stephen Oppenheimer, Gavin Menzies, Hector Holt-house, Xavier Herbert, M. Cannon, D. Harvey, Dr Errol West, Dr Gary Foley, Dr Rosalind Kidd, Dr A. Haebich, Dr E. McHugh, Dr N. Loos, Dr J. Garbarino, Dr Donald Thompson, Professor Ross Fitzgerald, Dr Lyndon Megarrity, Dr David Symons, Dr E. Leach, Dr G. Pike, H. Steven, Chloe Hooper, Daniel Miller, Christopher Tilley, J. W. Collinson, W. S. Oliver, David Moore, Rodney Hall, Alec Martin, Julie Martyn, Dr Bryce Barker, Dr David McKnight and Ron Edwards.

I offer special thanks for permission to reproduce images granted by the State Library of Victoria, The British Library Board, Laurel Hall of Rangeville, QLD and Cleveland Fagan.

All photos are by me, except where I have given credit to others. The dance shown on the back cover was at Laura Dance Festival. Those taken at Barron Falls, Stoney Creek Falls, Lockhart River, Windermere and Green Island are by unknown photographers. The 'stonefish' and 'man sitting on a crocodile' photos were taken about 1956 by the Cairns Postmaster whose name I have forgotten.

For the spelling of the names of Bama languages and nations I have adopted that used by Timothy Bottoms, except in direct quotes.

I refer to my sources like this (Surname, Date, Page) so you can look them up in the References at the end of the book.

Patsy Coverdale
Greensborough 2011

INTRODUCTION

North Queensland in Black and White—A social history with stories, views and archaeology is my explanation of relations between the Bama and Gadja people of North Queensland. Even after 200 years, not understanding each other still leads to clashes of culture—sometimes fruitful, sometimes violent.

My observations, over fifty years, start from my youth as a white girl in Redlynch near Cairns, where I got to know some of the Djabugay. I continued to observe during my regular returns to the North to visit friends and my parents, Alan and Hazel Pride.

Before White settlement, all the country on the coastal plain, the mountains and the tablelands gave life to and belonged to the Aboriginal people. By the 1950s, when I lived at Redlynch, the land under the cusp of the Kuranda Range was covered with sugar cane farms cut out of the rainforest. I went to hear the anthropologist C. P. Mountford, became a reporter on *The Cairns Post* and met and learnt from famous anthropologists. I began to study as an external student of the University of Queensland.

One summer day in 1955 I met Xavier Herbert, the extrovert White author, at Redlynch beneath the brows of the mountain. We stood at the edge of the crossroads where the grass grew out from the polished red concrete floors of the wide verandahs. Two Djabugay sat at a distance in the shade of the shop, quietly observing us. No cars passed us.

We chatted as the sun made pools of shade from our hats upon our shoulders. I said I was going to England for experience.

A thought passed between us: was I following his lead? Xavier had written *Capricornia* mostly in London before he achieved his fame as a novelist. Then he gave away why he campaigned passionately for Aborigines' sense of their place, their country, when he said to me,

'When I went to get a passport I found my birth, who my father was, had never been registered; I didn't exist.'

This was something he had in common with many Aborigines. He was in fact born in Western Australia and later came to the Cairns district. To learn about the world I spent four years in Europe, two working in public relations with Australia House in the United Kingdom. Then I lived at Oxford with my new husband from Yorkshire in a city full of treasures of history and archaeology. My husband Eric Coverdale was the Accelerator Technical Officer in the Nuclear Physics Research Department at the Clarendon Laboratory at Oxford University. Through him I learned a little science.

I came back to Australia with my husband and son and a wider world view, which included antiquity, physics, social studies and a new concept of culture. We had a second son. Eric rose to Chief Technical Officer at the Physics Department at Melbourne University.

Introduction

My father, Alan Pride with Xavier Herbert (right) at our house "Oroya" in Redlynch in 1954.
Photo by my mother, Hazel Nance Pride.

I became a reporter again, writing articles for newspapers and magazines in Australia and overseas. I was a member of the Inventors Association of Australia.

At La Trobe University, I learned more about social power, status, discrimination and the past and got a Bachelor of Arts in Sociology and Archaeology in 1994.

In this book, I will analyse the positions of Whites and Blacks, pointing to examples and research about how they get on, and how they fail to.

My Aboriginal friend looked up from an early draft of this book. 'It's all true', she said.

Prof Chris Anderson (head of Anthropology at the South Australian Museum) said to me:

> 'We need this book. It bridges the big gap between children's stories and tertiary studies. It develops source material resources of culture now dispersed. We need to document these for Aborigines and for people in general.'

Once when travelling on Skyrail to the top of Mount Williams, near Cairns, I took a photograph of the dense rainforest growing below me. When the photo was developed, I discovered that a lens flare had superimposed a luminous Rainbow Serpent image of shining energy.

I thought it was most appropriate since the Bama think of this mountain as their Serpent and as grandfather. Here was the radiant awesome sign of authority. I knew then what I had to do.

Introduction

The oldest continuous religious symbol, the Rainbow Serpent, remains to sustain Aboriginal people. They believe they are born from the spirit of the land and when they die they return to it.

Where there is no sign of green shoot, no ray of sun and the heavy silence of hearts breaking, know that behind the dark clouds waits a sacred presence whose domain is beyond trespass, with a sky legend that endures. Look beyond despair, otherwise in those black moments of depression other people's hearts are full of sorrow too. For each bleak moment you can find an enchanting flash of rainbow.

Another example of the divine power of a shining serpent to save its people from death is the biblical bronze serpent of Moses in *Numbers Chapter 21:7-9*.

The Rod of Asclepius with a serpent around a staff is a great symbol of healing adopted by the medical profession.

WORDS USED IN NORTH QUEENSLAND

AIATSIS	Australian Institute of Aboriginal and Torres Strait Islander Studies.
ATSIC	Australian and Torres Strait Islander Commission.
Bama	Rainforest aboriginal people of Far North of Queensland. See Map 1.
Bana Warru	Upper Barron River.
Buda:adji	The sacred carpet snake.
Bulmba	A habitable place or homeland.
Bulurru	The Bama ancestral culture of tribal law and religion which includes the Storywaters.
Damarri	An heroic mischievous Storywater character.
Darrella	An Aboriginal camp at Redlynch.
Din Din	Barron Falls.
Djabugay	A Bama tribe that lives on and around the mountain at Kuranda and below at Redlynch. Also their language. Also spelt 'Dgabugai' and 'Tjapukai'. See Map 2.
Djabuganydji	A person who speaks Djabugay, or a particular Djabugay dialect. Also spelt Dgabigannydji.

Words used in NQ

Gadja	The 'Spirit of a dead person', usually male. Bama used this term to refer to Europeans.
Guyala	An heroic good Storywater character, as opposed to Damarri.
Inside Storywaters	The Storywaters told to people who are initiated into their community.
Kamerunga	Lower Barron River.
Kanaka	A person with Melanesian Pacific Island ancestry.
Maladamban	An Aboriginal Sorcerer.
Murri	An aborigine from any of the many tribes in Queensland.
Outside Storywaters	The storywaters known by the initiated people, told to uninitiated members of the Murri community and may be sold in tourist shops.
Quinkan	A thin invisible spirit with sorcery powers.
Rainbow Serpent	The Creation Ancestor depicted as a carpet snake.
Sahul land	New Guinea, mainland Australia and Tasmania linked as one landmass during the Pleistocene era, when the sea levels were approximately 150 metres lower than they are today.
Skin story	Family history of the Murri people.

Storywaters	Ancestral morality tales which focus on specific places, explain the origins of landforms, cultural practices and their worldview. These give the Murri a moral order which frames their existence.
Wayan	A cleverman amongst the Murri people.
Yarrabah	The Church of England mission for Aboriginal people who had been captured and relocated to Yarrabah settlement, across Trinity Bay Inlet from Cairns.
Yirrganydji	People of the coast. Also spelt Yirrikandji and Irukandji.

LIST OF ILLUSTRATIONS

Alan Pride with Xavier Herbert	3
Map Legend	11
Map 1: Far North Queensland	12
Map 2: Djabugay Country	13
Portrait at Endeavour River	14
Descending to the coast on Skyrail	17
Harvesting sugar cane	40
Steam train climbing Mount Williams	43
The train at Stoney Creek Falls	44
Barron Falls	46
Cane fire across the railway line	47
A stone fish	49
The Cairns Post	51
A gold prospecting shaft at Darrella	52
Patsy, Zelda and schoolchildren at Yarrabah	57
Lunchtime in the playground at Yarrabah	58
Stephen and Mona Fagan	60
Stephen and Mona's home at Oak Forest	64
Getting ready to dance at Yarrabah	70
Kelvin Hill at Tully	72
Barron River tribesman	94
Roy and Don Banning	102

Lockhart River mission women	106
Underwater coral garden observatory	149
Lloyd Grigg with crocodile skin and eggs	150
Patsy preparing to dive	151
Crocodile and hunter	156
Roger Cribb near Ngarrabullgan	158
Bromfield Swamp	159
Buttercup Banning	161
Pam Oui demonstrates stone axes	166
A bark coolamon displaying seeds	168
A nut-grinding stone	169
A Green Island reef at low tide	176
Patsy on the Big Cat, Green Island	195

Illustrations

• CAIRNS	Town (selected)
WHITE ROCK	Feature (selected)
KUKU YALANJI	Language
Yirrganydji	Nation
....	Language boundary
—+—+—+—+—+—	Railway
————————	Waterbody
————————	Reef
————————	Coast
— — — — — —	500m interval contour
▲1068	Spot height

Topographic data from 1:250,000 map
Geoscience Australia www.ga.gov.au.
Language and nation data from maps
by Timothy Bottoms (1992).
Maps created using Terramodel software.

Map Legend

NQ in Black and White

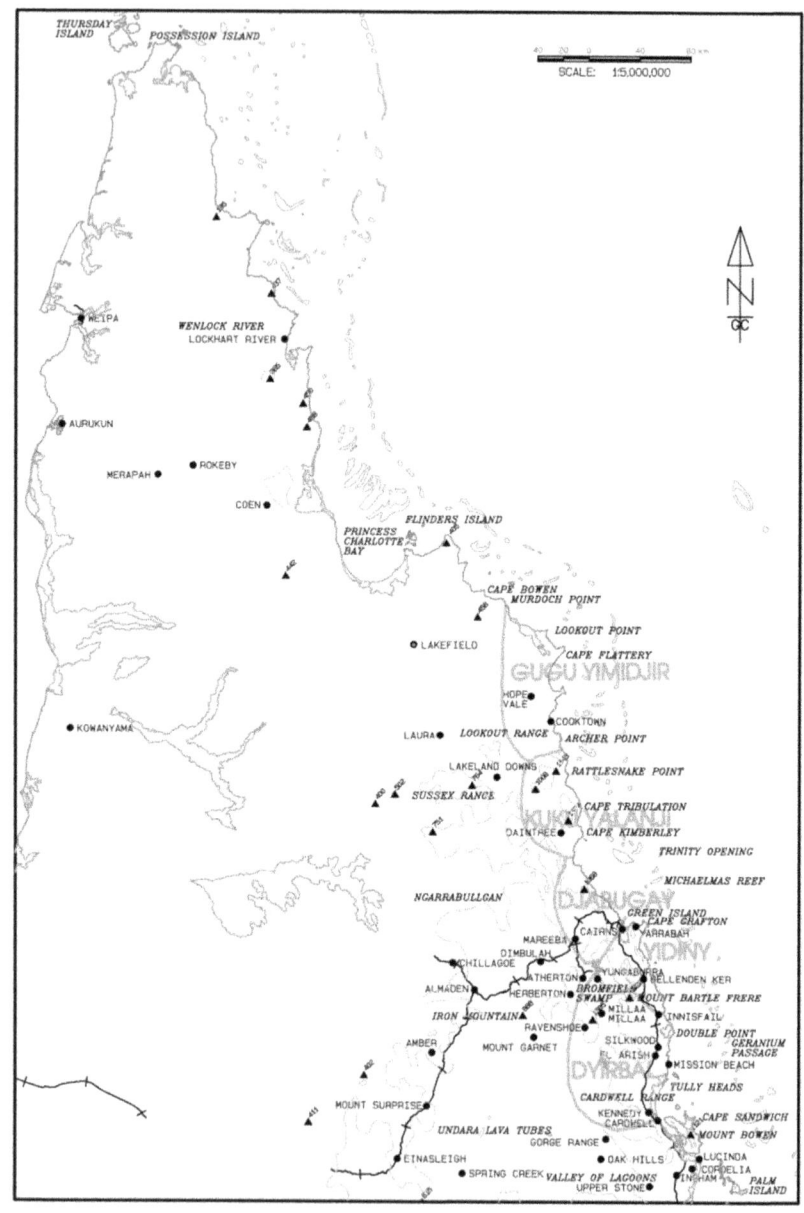

Map 1: Far North Queensland

Map 2: Djabugay Country

NQ in Black and White

Portrait of an Australian Aborigine made at the Endeavour River.
Copy by Charles Praval of a lost drawing, probably by Sydney Parkinson in 1770 or 1771.
© The British Library Board Add.15508 f.13. All Rights Reserved.

CHAPTER 1
HOME ON THE MOUNTAIN

Both men felt the fate of the country was in their hands. The Aborigine grasped a bunch of leaves to ward off the evil spirits and held a spear to his side. The white artist sat sketching him eagerly, silently, with his pencil. A menacing omen of conflict lurked behind the compassionate picture.

The Aborigine was poised, curious but courageous, for he alone had remained near the ship's crew. He was a wayan, a sorcerer, who sought to use his renowned spell against the foreigners. The white artist was Sydney Parkinson from HMS *Endeavour*, commanded by Lieutenant James Cook. *Endeavour* had been holed on coral in 1770 and had been beached for repairs at what we now call Endeavour River, Cooktown, Far North Queensland. Fascinated yet afraid, Parkinson (1784/1984), kept drawing the first portrait on paper of a Cape York Aboriginal man.

The portrait speaks volumes—but did the sorcerer's spell succeed? Parkinson died soon after, in Batavia in the East Indies. These two brave young men were from different worlds. Eventually representatives of each world would show each other how to survive in North Australia.

In the settlement of tropical North Queensland, both Blacks and Whites sensed the mountain range's power to make them feel strong; they are drawn back to the coast and hills. Along with the media discourse, the bush yarn, tribal myths and the oral sagas called 'Storywaters', are other tales waiting to be heard, some are inscribed on paper, stone, bone or skin.

There are many folk tales of domestic life, but the official histories of these private ways have often left out the Murris, to use an Indigenous name for Queensland Aboriginal people. In this book, we will look at the issues they are facing: their lives, the historical background, their sociology and prehistory.

To heal the hearts of today we need to hear about the pain of yesterday, even if it makes people so anxious they cannot speak about the pain caused by the racial conflicts. It won't go away; it just sits there like skin cancer. It's about who owns ideas, who says we can speak, about what and how, and language as a tool of racism and control. Healing the wounds leaves scars.

When these truths about the struggle are written, people in the stories may feel stripped bare, left without their own comfortable justifying tone. If you see the name of a dead person for whom you grieve in this book, please bear with me and turn the page, for their sake.

Non-Aboriginal people like me are still evolving their own national myth of an urban coastal culture which will help to endure the effects of globalisation and give them a voice in it.

Home on the mountain

Descending to the coast on Skyrail

Murris too want to define the terms of the shared inhabitation of the land rather than have an adversarial relationship with which to embrace nationhood. The Murris that I know would like effective ways to do this. We have to dream heroism onward into a new industry of positive voices.

At the cusp of Mount Williams we are either up or down or going to be. The fragrant flowers, the abundant wet plants and trees, all rotting down and bursting into life, make an unforgettable smell. When we go across the crest of the mountain down to the humid coast the air is like our warm breath hovering. Today we can walk or drive, or fly overhead by Skyrail cable car, to look down on the wonder of the rainforest.

The long folds of the Macalister Range bask in the blazing sun under the bluest of skies like a great carpet snake. The first people here felt it was part of their family, the Rainbow Serpent, the Grandfather. Rainforest clothed the outstretched folds. The slopes were a mysterious mantle within which the people sheltered each night. As the sun went down in a fiery crimson show, darkness dropped down. The fireflies glowed magically among the trees and vines, drifting silently into the gunyahs (palm leaf huts). Later the settlers would see this too, the shining drift of tiny living lights into the houses and the mosquito nets, every Wet season. That's really how it was.

The Djabugai are the tribe who live on and around the mountain at Kuranda and below at Redlynch. Today they are custodians of traditions, anxieties and politics, both old and new. Bama is the name for rainforest Aboriginal people in the Far North including the Djabugai.

While some of them liked to keep to themselves, small bands exchanged foods, artefacts, ideas and marriage partners to survive; the resourceful Bama developed the performing arts to exchange with people from the open country. This flowers today as the Tjapukai Aboriginal Cultural Park on the coast at Smithfield where you join the Skyrail Scenic Railway. There you can see a long running dance performance, examine tools and try your hand with a boomerang, a spear and a didgeridoo.

One hot summer afternoon many years ago, as I rode my bicycle past their settlement at Darrella at Redlynch, I saw a Bama couple sitting in the shade of the cane train bridge. They were leaning back on its heavy timbers and were surveying the bright red soil, the stands of sugar cane resplendent with their flowering plumes stirring lightly in the breeze, and the jungly mountains beyond. There they felt cool away from their tin cottage. Their stories seemed to be rising languidly in the afternoon haze and I wanted to hear them, for our 'Firefly Country' was like no other.

Their histories have a place and take time to happen, to be told, to be treasured intimately. Without their natural element the people fear their spiritual character, and thousands of years and their triumphs and tragedies, will be lost.

Their Bulurru is the Bama ancestral culture of tribal law and religion. The Bama practised their Bulurru while they were moving through their homeland, their Bulmba, according to the seasons. They used to move through the mountains and valleys, and streams and on to the plains. Their 'Storywaters' about this way of life presented the past as a set of dramas which gave relevance to a moral order to frame existence (Bottoms, 1990, p. 50). It provided models of behaviour for the tribes to flourish. This is so for all the Bama, including the Yirrganydji, Yidinji, Gungganydji, Buluwanydji, Muluridji and Kuku Yalanji. There are many other tribes in the Storywaters country of Far North Queensland.

The first people to come to the north-east coast of Australia were the Bama. They called the White latecomers 'Gadja', which can mean 'spirit of a dead person', or 'white devil'. The Whitefellas called the natives 'niggers.'

To find their way up the seemingly impenetrable ranges, Whitefellas watched the Djabugay come and go across the pass; three white men and two Djabuganydji conquered those ramparts on 19 September 1876 (Pike, 1956, p. 5). The Whites and Blacks slowly learned another world view from each other. By 1891, the Europeans had built a railway up the mountain range to the Atherton Tablelands and the pass became Number Ten Tunnel on the railway.

Today the paths under the canopy of spreading trees are traversed by both the Gadja and the Bama in a journey of reconciliation. It can be hard to determine who can claim which rights. Practical arrangements for traditions, for camping and businesses coexist. The high slopes above the railway line are Crown land, largely a magnificent national park. The land below is privately owned with housing and tourism, rapidly replacing cane farming. Some Aboriginal areas and sacred sites are preserved; there is a native title claim for the park.

The Europeans did not recognise the territorial boundaries of the Aboriginal tribes. In social groups there were, and are, vertical boundaries as well as horizontal ones. These boundaries are about culture as well as economic status. The land claims are about more than land use and ownership. They are about boundaries of Them and Us, power and status, languages and beliefs.

Boundaries and power were tested on the banks of the river in June 1770 when *Endeavour* was beached to save it from the Great Barrier Reef.

On a calm moonlit evening, Cook and his crew were in their bunks at eleven o'clock. Their ship ground on to a coral reef with a terrifying sound. Cook wrote in his journal:

'We were upon sunken coral rocks, the most dreadful of all on account of their sharp points and grinding quality, which cut through the ship's bottom almost immediately' (Wood, 1970, p. 96).

The ship and its men were kept afloat by holding the coral and the fothering sail in the hole. After manoeuvring the ship onto shore, all the sailors were safe and exhausted.

Trouble ensued over a fair exchange of goods from *Endeavour's* crew with the tribe of Aboriginal people. Cook had not given to them two of the twelve turtles his men caught, when they asked for the turtles. He had used his nets in their fishing zone (Bottoms, 1990, p. 146). Instead he had offered biscuits. They retaliated by burning one of his tents on the shore (Fitzgerald et al., 2009, p. 9).

Despite this conflict, Cook wrote in his journal that he thought the Aboriginal people at the Endeavour River 'were in reality far more happier than we Europeans without the necessary conveniences so much sought after in Europe' (Wood, 1970, p. 102).

The concept of founding homelands emboldened explorers to go to other places to make their fortune. To have resources and power in their own hands rather than dispute them, they went to unsettled frontiers. The colonists were driven by their Western myth that all development was sustainable; that is, other forms of life would also continue to go on. They also believed sons and daughters would labour with them, or they might make a life for themselves over the horizon. Today we can go by plane over far horizons.

Events like the Mount Williams air disaster in 1991 opened up a common dialogue between the two races in the Cairns area. The Bama elders believed that bad fortune follows desecration of sacred country; to trespass on Rainbow Serpent air space would be fatal. The ominous low cloud round the peaks is the magic sign for DANGER; DO NOT ENTER; ENTER AT OWN RISK for both the Bama and for the aeroplane pilots. The Mayor of Cairns and four city councillors were killed on the high rainforest slopes.

Both groups are awed by the land and its productive power, recognising it as a type of currency. White societies gained technical development and knowledge of control through eras of settlement instead of always moving on. Farming surpluses had produced social power and time to develop ideas. Infrastructure was built, and thought of as permanent assets. People who did not think like this were called 'savages'. European settlers wanted such benefits to be exchanged for the land they desired.

Murris already had their own protective social contract of intertribal laws and land use. The Aboriginal men, women and children maintained a hunter-gatherer universe, of abundance in the Dry season, and big-seed grinding in the Wet season. They went down to the lowlands in the Dry, then into the uplands after the first storms of the Wet, in what Whites called December.

Etiquette of positive exchange, tribal courtesy and consensus or pay-back violence prevailed for the Bama. They had no concept of rank, servant or master, unlike the colonists. Formally they gave their name and expected the names of the men presenting themselves. The acknowledgment of entering a tribal territory was, and still is, an important protocol for all Aboriginal peoples today.

In their philosophy of knowledge, the Bama named all the categories found within the boundaries of their experience to give them their reality, their character. The Bama named parts of the body intentionally. Because of their sense of power over natural phenomena they took responsibility for their Bulmba, their homeland. They signified this in their naming and their dancing, which showed their respect for the animals and birds that once were people. Mona Fagan, a Bama lady, explained that the name 'Djabugay' means 'where is your home, your humpy?' as from the question 'dja bayung bayu?' (where is the place to go fishing?).

When they staged ceremonies, the Bama tribes brought into their existence the kangaroos, turtles, crocodiles, fruit bats, lizards, fish and food trees. The ritual activity was the work.

The Bama did not at first see that European 'work' congealed into money to exchange for the material production of their 'goods', their 'cargo'. Instead, the Bama made careful drawings of nature, for the naming of their world's parts represented the critical tribal control device over creation. They listened for European names because they thought that using the correct name and ritual would bring forth European goods (Bottoms, 1990, p. 47).

The Gungu Yimidhirr iconic naming power is still present in their word 'kangaroo', the national symbol. At Endeavour River in the north in 1770, this name was recorded by James Cook and Joseph Banks. Later it was repeated by Arthur Phillip in Sydney Cove to Aboriginal people there. The Sydney Cove Aboriginals did not know the word's meaning.

Aboriginal people's contact with the Gadja meant the younger people could break away from the older men, who had traditionally been all powerful in the tribe. The knowledge of the

Law and traditions had been in the elders' custody and they refused, or were not asked, to pass it on. In Bama terms the youth were not 'ready'; the young people thought that old elemental skills and magic must be past their 'use-by' date.

The Bama had already achieved a native cyclical economy in their own park environment. Their control of food resources was not apparent to the European settlers, and neither was their practice of carefully burying human waste to prevent sorcery. The Bama believed they were in charge of the future, making them centuries ahead of their time. Will we all be 'ready', or 'savage' as on Easter Island, when the land is past its 'use-by' date?

Belonging to the country you inhabit means grasping that spellbinding bunch of leaves, owning its romantic images and violent history.

The name 'Australia', with all its character, came to the explorer-navigator Matthew Flinders as he surveyed the coast of the Great South Land in 1803. He could see Aboriginal people who also create identities with names.

CHAPTER 2
THE ROMANCE BETWEEN CULTURES

The sun sets with sheets of gold and fiery crimson behind the mountain peak; it gets dark quickly. In the dusk the traffic, the sounds of the day, quieten. While the birds roost and twitter, and fruit bats fly off to find food, the palm leaves sigh, and the flowing water murmurs. The sounds of the night begin; cicadas sing. Some cities have lost these magical moments.

The Bama lawyer cane and grass humpies, which were illuminated by the campfire, where the families gathered to eat and to plan the next day, have been replaced. Instead of serenity there is noise.

In a Cairns night spot, the worries of the day are pushed aside into the dark by loud music. There is no fire, no hearth. Campfire cosiness is copied by a projected photographic scene and some flickering coloured lights. The young people sit on chairs, all modern, or dance in courtship rituals, as old as the ancestors, in the late hours when families are asleep. A tribal dancing ceremony here would be a sacrilege.

Men take the lead. Women fix their face painting. With liquor they are brave and jolly. They are trying to get close to someone, anyone. They may feel loved, intimate, and happy; they try to hold on to this trust, this treasure they want to grasp.

On a tall stool, a dark lissom young woman sits, quietly defensive, her crinkly curled hair firmly held in place; she is a Bama with mixed-race heritage, her face and neat figure a portrait of her past. She shares her blended heritage with her partner, a very handsome youth who leans on the bar. He is a man; he has money and a can of drink and he says nothing.

Suddenly he turns away from the young woman, 'I don't know who my father is. He's English. I don't need him!' The fierce denial strikes like a knife, a heart-breaking script for the great Australian loneliness. What is really going on? I think our young people, with happy moments together and then crying privately in their rage and pain, are like a national de-facto marriage.

I grieve for his need to be held by his father, to be loved. Both sons and daughters deserve to blossom confidently in the care and guidance of their loving father and his family. But the young woman is doing what she can. He will need her touch, her sensuous pleasure and her laughing with him, her mothering. She will listen to his triumphs and tragedies. Perhaps he will listen to hers, will give those homely small attentions we get from parents, of which the Bama were deprived.

This young man is struggling to enter an alien dominant culture, hoping for wealth and power in his own hands. His hollow feelings of loss pursue him like his shadow. His father and grandfather may not know he is alive. They have lost their connection to the future, their immortality beyond their reach. Their fathers and grandfathers could have been men passing through, not knowing where life was taking them. We can see men like them in the sketch-book *The Australian Yarn* (Edwards, 1996, pp. 182–183), throwing a bottle out from a Kuranda train. Are they the missing piece of the national jigsaw puzzle?

That Bama girl has courage; she joins two worlds. Both cultures are circling round each other, fascinated, not knowing how to make the right move, to make it happen when the spirit moves.

Believing who you come from and where you belong is the foundation of personal security, to relate to others with confidence and power. We can find role models to lead us forward, like Murri lawyer, Noel Pearson, who articulates the issues and suggests constructive solutions to complex problems. As leader of the Cape York Tribal Council he said,

> 'Seeing ourselves as victims doesn't work anymore; that means we are not. Human beings who grasp for peace out of the turmoil of ordinary rather frantic relationships are wrestling to remodel transactions of power'.

The Cape York Tribal Council defends what it has retained of its traditional culture and native title rights. The power of the Council has grown on the peninsula with the decline of missions and the development of mining. Mr Pearson has struggled for years with the issue of Aboriginal sovereignty. In his lecture on 'Aboriginality on Globalisation', at the 1997 conference Globalising Australia at La Trobe University in Bundoora, Mr Pearson said,

> 'Settling the land rights issue can be done in due course ungrudgingly, finding principles of sharing the country. In Australia individuals on both sides require a fidelity gesture. We need to identify disinterest and ideology in these affairs. All Australia will suffer if the Racial Discrimination Act is diminished. We have the one opportunity in centuries and the subtlety, skill and judgment to make a go of reconciliation, to take courage and rekindle our aspirations, for the Mabo and

> Wik judgments are civilising moments in our constitutional history.

> 'Some ask is the hostility which is brought about too great a cost to continue? Here we can employ that subtlety, skill and judgment by realising that when attacked we defend our position more forcefully. When confronted, human beings strengthen the very beliefs their adversaries are challenging. When both tribes use the adversarial approach, it guarantees sabre and spear rattling.

> 'Issues of power arise when people pose a threat. Primary producers see settled land use as vital to the economy and that Aborigines did and would do nothing with it; seasonal occupation is, well, Dreaming. Murris like the feel of the land and the smell of the bush but they like the feel of a dry roof, a cold beer, a warm blanket and their civil rights as much as "white" people do. The Anglo myth that they will die out or fade away into coloured servants is as valid as the Aboriginal myth that the Whites will pack up and go back to England. The white people have accumulated rights over the years and they are staying, despite pastoral and farming grieving over loss of the easy pre-Mabo times. Simplistic policies will leave both tribes, both nations, powerless, defenceless and without international allies.'

At the Cape York Partnership Business Summit, on 27 August, 2000, Mr Pearson said,

> 'Murris need business and management skills for a quiet revolution after three decades of passive welfare. We don't think hard enough about living at the bottom of the safety net of social services. We should be defending our people's rights to a better place in the economy, to self-sufficiency. With our

two per cent of the population we are forty per cent of the prison population which includes violence among our families. There is a more urgent need to confront drug and grog consumption, ours being perhaps the highest in the world. We should restore social control; addiction is not inevitable. We may need restrictions. Our old ladies checking on youths at night is a sign of confronting the problems.

'I speak for Cape York with community leaders, with more of this needing to be done. We need an economic stake in the country to climb out of our dependency.'

Ideologies are adopted by groups quietly to protect and control their methods. Our national disquiet is complex, fraught with contradictions. In 1959, the 45,010 Indigenous people living in Queensland were very marginalized, with over 17,000 classified as 'controlled', the Queensland Government retaining part of their low wages in 'trust accounts' (Fitzgerald et al., 2009, p. 140).

It took until early 2003 to finalise a $54 million compensation package for the thousands of Indigenous workers entitled to claim lost wages (Fitzgerald, 2009, p. 168). As a result of the Commonwealth Intervention in Aboriginal communities, and Indigenous efforts to repossess their traditional lands, the Aboriginal people have become more politically aware. They are struggling to deconstruct colonialism in their minds.

CHAPTER 3
THE URBAN JUNGLE

It is two hours' walk inland from Cairns to the real rainforest on the sacred mountains. Now you can fly over it. Many people are drawn to the coast of Far North Queensland. International airline traffic has transformed its economy. The aeroplanes have brought worldliness with them, with its opportunities and threats, new ways and new diseases.

In the Deep North since World War II, the introduction of highways, airports, insecticide, computers, telephones and television changed life forever. Industrial development and modern infrastructure have grown alongside primary industries. A multicultural tourist paradise economy for visitors has required external norms and values. These have conflicted with the conservative cultural character the long-term residents have tried to preserve, both Bama and Gadja.

For the tourists, there are the casino, the hotels, the golf course, the parking meters, the court house, the prison and the theme park. Furthermore, a beach on the palm-fringed esplanade has replaced the mangroves. Now tourists can all frolic free and safe and warm in a seaside lagoon in the heart of the amenities!

The twinkling of fireflies once lit up the mountain's rainforest. Since the redevelopment, we can see sparkle in the tropical undergrowth, but it is now electronic: lights for casino tourists in a rooftop garden under a translucent dome. This beautiful display of greenery has a stage for performers, which presents a convincingly natural and ordered setting. The performers included Murris. This casino stage is an icon of the rapid social transformation of the

White culture as well as an Indigenous one. The White elite are made the centre of social control while Murris' beliefs are not mentioned.

When the chips are down, a family just likes a picnic under a few palm trees. I saw a Bama mother handing round a drink from a plastic bottle, in waxed paper beakers to the children. They were squatting quietly under the shade of a Travellers' palm on pension day.

That palm tree scene, with its Bama mother and her three kids, said it all. They were gambling, really taking quite a trick, making a native title claim, because they were in the city centre, two blocks away from the casino, behind a concrete shelter on the nature strip. I was passing them in a taxi. It was not the postcard image. As the heat of the day began to rise, people began to move about the wide shaded footpaths to the shops in the delightful Cairns ambience, of which we were all a part.

The taxi driver drove me round this scene again to show me what Cairns could be like; to him the family was a unit of the angst and disagreement the whole nation has been trying to resolve.

He said, 'They are like children with money. They share it round with their relatives and provide for the day; when it's gone someone else will get a bit and on they go. They sleep under the trees along the shore. I often drive them to Yarrabah especially when they have been drinking. A female welfare worker from the South got talking after a few drinks the other night.'

The taxi driver repeated the welfare worker's words. 'She said, "They are unfairly treated and so misunderstood". I put down

The urban jungle

my glass and replied, "You go home then with them and sympathise. Be kind. While they are drinking they are like cannibals and you will probably be raped. Then tell me." '

There it was again—his normalising the problems between Blacks and Whites, expecting that the Government should take responsibility for the past. While dispossession for anyone creates inexpressible self-destruction, those who work and pay tax to support the system feel outraged, attacked by those who feel powerless inside it.

Towns can be a social wilderness in psychological terms. Do you make this wilderness your home? There are rapes in the parks and on the foreshore. For some the urban jungle can be an untamed world. Both Black and White people have changed their popular culture because the other one has been there. Magistrate Ms Pat O' Shane has had to face this challenge as an Aboriginal person. In 2001, she said to me,

> 'Once we have changed, we have changed forever. It's like the loss of innocence. We can't forget our experiences. It's like wishing my nephew Tjandamurra had never been burnt'.

[The six-year-old boy was set alight in a Cairns North school yard in 1996 by a White man.]

In deconstructing the cultures jostling together on the foreshores, and at the social service offices, there could be a slippage of concepts we cannot quite grasp. But ideology can be detected, even if it is juggling invisible attitudes. Like us seeking answers, some social scientists want things they can hold and measure, not ideas invented by theory (Leach, 1976, p. 4), so they use money exchanges (the congealed-labour symbol) to calculate this.

Now, managing money takes quite a lot of practice. Murris need more than the smell of it; they need the feel of it, the responsibility and consequences of its abstract economic power. Non-Aboriginal players have shown just how hard it can be to feel and handle money in the ideology of a public place such as a picnic ground.

Anzac Park in Cairns was a sacred memorial to war heroes beside Trinity Bay. The Bama gathered there regularly under the Poinciana trees. They were trying to accommodate a dominant culture but keep their own Law, with the mix of tribal, rural and urban families in their diaspora. They were overruled by the quest for tourist dollars and asked to gather elsewhere; the heroes who fought for our liberty saw the Bama priced out of it. The Casino was built on the park, an icon of Cairns development.

CHAPTER 4
KEEPING RECORDS

International lawyer Friedrich Carl Von Savigny wrote, in *Treatise on Possession* in the early years of the nineteenth century:

> '1. Possession is the foundation of property;
>
> 2. Presence on the spot [which] enables [the occupant] not merely to walk over every individual portion of it but to deal with it in any way he chooses at pleasure. Personal presence is then the fundamental first step in acquiring possession' (Reynolds, 1996, p. 47).

As the *Cooktown Herald* of 24 June 1874 saw it, when savages are pitted against civilisation they must go to the wall; it is the fate of their race. Much as we may deplore such a view, it was considered absolutely necessary that the march of civilisation not be arrested by the antagonism of the Aboriginals (Fitzgerald et al., 2009, p. 33).

The oral histories, the remains of tracks and mountain passes, and material culture in metal, stone and bone, are testimony to the struggle for domination of the territory. 'In clashes one may examine policies of different past periods, the consciousness of those in power and of the subordinates ... This representation (of the cultural world) constitutes a transformation of the world in the direction of those interests' (Miller & Tilley, 1984, pp. 12–14). In other words, ideologies are used by groups to protect and control their ways.

Today, Mount Williams is seen from above the ancestral heights in the carriages of Skyrail, where one gazes down on a luxuriant rainforest canopy or cleared areas. In frontier days it was not tourism territory. The young Australian government just wanted to conquer it, to rearrange the inhabitants much as they wanted to rearrange the bush. At that time, the thick jungle in the valleys and on the mountain slopes was a fortress where the Bama found refuge from the invading white settlers. Introduced horses and cattle could not go into the rainforest. Furthermore, the Bama could move through the forest using the safe highways provided by the headwaters of the creeks and rivers near each other in the mountain range. These paths were unknown to the newcomers.

The war between the native occupants and the whites was, then, a fight to take control of resources. From the earliest recorded encounter at Battle Creek in 1870 both sides were on the lookout against one another.

> 'One peculiarity of the natives was their aversion to visiting certain parts of the coast. Rev E. R. Gribble mentions two places which were carefully avoided; part of the Cape Grafton coast, and the Red Cliffs beyond Double Island Point. In any case the scrub-dwelling blacks were inclined to avoid the open country, except on hunting and fishing excursions. Their sheltering gunyahs or mia-mias were generally built in a forest "pocket" at the edge of the scrub and not far from fresh water.
>
> 'Those tribes inhabiting the low lands on the inlet, and Mulgrave and Russell Rivers were fairly numerous, they were not given to tribal war, and lived in fairly large "towns". They built substantial canoes, which must have entailed long and arduous labour in hollowing out a cedar log by alternately burning and chipping out with stone tools. The fracas at Bat-

tle Creek in 1870 was ascribed to the theft of one of these canoes. Later a prominent Government official at Cooktown publicly stated that if the people at Cairns had trouble with the natives it could be traced back to that event. He went further in his statement and said if the people did not secure the help of the blacks in the menial work of the settlement it would be their own fault' (Collinson, 1939, p. 61).

It was all about having legitimate property and resources to survive. The local newspapers and journals of their time provide an open window on the difficulties and opportunities then and a graphic record of racial and survival attitudes, on the haemorrhaging history. The first skirmish of many between armed parties took place on a track up the Barron River. A report in *The Port Denison Times*, Cairns, 25 November, 1876, concluded:

> 'Since this first brush I understand the blacks have been twice interviewed by the same party, and that on each occasion there was an interchange of compliments, without any casualties, however, on the side of the white men.'

In 1882, a journalist from *The Sydney Morning Herald* spent a day with a small group of Djabuganydji in their rainforest.

> 'It is difficult to get food', they told him. 'The whites have taken all the good country. We have to go to the mountains, to the no good country, the rocky coast near the Yirrikandji where fish is not plentiful' (Reynolds, 1982, p. 114).

A Barron River selector, E. C. Putt, wrote in a letter that was published on 30 July 1885 in the *Herberton Advertiser* about black raids on his property.

'I deem it my duty to make it known to intending settlers the losses through blacks I have suffered during the present year when on January 12th they visited my property and were shot at leaving a dilly bag and bone bodkin, used for husking corn, behind them. On the 13th they again stole corn... on nine occasions between the 12th January and 5th April the niggers stole corn. On 14th April, 23rd and 30th May, and 4th June, they stole corn. Of four acres planted in July, I gathered ten bushels, off four acres planted in November six bushels and off two acres in January I got nothing. The niggers had the rest. They have now started removing English potatoes and pumpkin' (Reynolds, 1982, p. 184).

Firepower prevailed. The most infamous raid occurred at Speewah, the selection John Atherton had taken up in 1877 at Emerald End near Mareeba, where his cattle ate native pasture. Ten years later displaced Bama had, it was said, agreed to drove a herd of cattle over the Douglas track in exchange for a bullock. Then he gave them a horse to bake in a 'bangarr', an earth oven. Being so hungry, the Bama set about cooking the beast at once.

It was then that Buttercup Banning, a young girl, burnt her hand and was taken by a woman to the river to cool it and to have a drink. While at the river they heard the guns crack and saw the massacre of their families by Native Mounted Police. They fled down the mountain to Crystal Cascades. The Black Water Lagoon massacre remained an unreported incident from the district of Wright's Crossing (Bottoms, 1995, p. 5). We will meet Buttercup again in Chapter 21.

On the Thornborough Road, the blacks were violent in places, notably at the 'Middle Crossing' (Kuranda). In 1879, George the Greek, a well-known packer, travelled seven miles to

Grove's shanty in the open country near the Clohesy River, with several spears in his legs, after losing all his packhorses and their loading. A Chinese storekeeper was killed at Granite Creek and the store looted. John Atherton at Emerald End suffered the loss of cattle and horses. At the Daintree, a timber-getter, Handley, and his mate started out on a trip with stores for another camp in the scrub, leaving his wife and a Kanaka at their own camp. When they did not return in a couple of days, and the other men were forced to come in for tucker, a search was made, resulting in the discovery of the mutilated bodies of the two men (Collinson, 1939, p. 63).

By this time there were 700 Gadja settlers, three males to every female, on the plains and hinterland. Then gold was discovered on the Etheridge, the Palmer and the Hodgkinson Rivers. Miners rushed to Cooktown and the district to try their luck until the gold ran out.

Among them were about 17,000 Chinese migrants, many of whom left to begin farming on the coast and the Atherton Tablelands in the late 1870s. By 1886 they had developed an important export crop of bananas for southern markets. Some 10,000 hectares under bananas are now grown, mainly in the Innisfail–Tully district and they are worth over $2,000,000 a year to the local economy (Oliver, 2002, p. 28).

The grass with sugar juice, native to Java and parts of New Guinea, and known to the Romans, was first grown near Brisbane in 1863 by Captain Louis Hope. By 1870 there were several mills in North Queensland (Oliver, 2002, p. 10). In 1879, a syndicate of Chinese farmers established the Hop Wah plantation to grow sugar cane on a 240 hectare crop five kilometres south of Cairns, at

Harvesting sugar cane at Redlynch

what is now Earlville. They also grew other tropical crops (Oliver, 2002, pp. 3–4).

The Pyramid Mill Estate on the Mulgrave River had over 5,000 acres of rich scrub land. In 1884, labour on this plantation consisted of thirty-five Europeans, eighty-one Kanakas and 100 Chinese to treat ten tons of cane per hour (Oliver, 2002, p. 28).

Much of the hard work of harvesting was being done by South Sea Islanders, the Kanakas, who were brought in by 'blackbirder' vessels and housed poorly.

As the number of plantations and imported labour increased, the Federal Government was under pressure to enact the 'White Australia' policy.

By 1900 the local government was repatriating most of the Pacific Islanders by force. Their entry was prohibited after March 1904. In 1907, 10,780 Kanakas were repatriated. However, some remained in Australia with homes and families, which drove the government to improve their conditions. They were paid six pounds per year plus food and clothing at a cost of about twenty-seven pounds by 1912 (Oliver, 2002, p. 10).

As the machine age pushed ahead, farmers began using tractors and listening to the news. The awareness of the north's vulnerability in national security was growing. When World War II came, the trusty tractor became crucial for defence work, building roads, airfields and depots.

In 1989, Murris were ordered off Elizabeth Henry's former property, Bellenden, near Tully, while collecting clay from a river bank to colour their paints. Later, it came to light that the property had been left to two Aboriginal stockmen, Spider and George Henry, by their white foster mother, cattle baroness Elizabeth Henry, when she died in 1961.

Due to a mistake in processing her will and the resistance from descendants, the 44.5 hectare property passed to the Uniting Church. The church sold it, but has since paid $110,000 in compensation to the men's family. Spider died in 1993, after he had finally learned that he had been left land, livestock, horses and saddlery by his adoptive mother.

Elizabeth Henry was a single World War I nurse who had inherited properties from her brother and sisters. Elizabeth respected her stockmen and the Aboriginal people of the area. Spider was the last full-blooded Aborigine of North Queensland's Jerrabel tribe and he shared the inheritance with Elizabeth's nephew. It included Top Paddock, which she had called 'John O'Groats'. It was the most northerly of Elizabeth Henry's three rich grazing and caneland properties (Easdown, 2002, p22).

As farms were established on the coast and tablelands, the railway slowly made its way from the coast up to Kuranda in the mountains by using the rainforest ramparts, on the pathway of Budaaji, the sacred Storywater carpet snake. The Djabugay raided the rail navvies' stores eventually but they were poisoned by rat-bait in damper (Bottoms, 1995, p. 5). The railway was completed in 1891. This was followed by a great flood on the Bana Warru (Upper Barron River), no doubt seen as Rainbow Serpent work by the Bama. The world-famous railway is now carrying trains decorated as Budaaji to the delight of its passengers.

The three-foot-six gauge railway, with its fifteen tunnels and over forty bridges, was the vital supply line to the Atherton Tablelands and the inland beyond. My family lived beside the line where the climb began at Redlynch.

Its secret charm for me, waking each morning, was to hear the steam engine preparing for its great work of climbing the many folds of the range with its load of freight and passengers.

Keeping records

Hazel Pride. *Steam train climbing Mount Williams, Redlynch.* 1957.

The train at Stoney Creek Falls

It would huff, chuff and cough, building up steam in the coal-fired boiler and then go along the triangle and the turntable with squeals of the turning wheels, then gasps of steam as it reached pressure for the climb. It would let out a shriek, and a triumphal whistle would echo through the gorge.

The Upper Barron River begins some kilometres from Kuranda and is called 'Buna' by the Bama. The area around the great falls is called 'Din Din'. The name gives a picture of its natural force because it means 'cyclone' or 'like an angry man'.

The force of the water in Australia's highest falls can be seen in what happened in the incident concerning Robert Philp of Burns Philp and Co. The 6,000-year-old yellow walnut tree found near the mouth of the river would never have survived a ride over the mighty falls. We know because in 1883 Robert Philp floated 15 million feet of red cedar logs down from Atherton, not knowing of the mighty drop, which smashed them to smithereens (Martin, p. 20). It was Australia's greatest timber smash. Fragments of cedar remain today high in crevices below the falls

Huge cedar and kauri pine trees were being dragged out of the forests and sawed up in timber mills in the early days. Ravenshoe had more than thirty bullock teams engaged transporting logs to be floated on rivers, or later, moved by steam train. Redlynch had its own timber mill, like many other settlements.

Barron Falls

Keeping records

The sugar industry became well established by 1880. The farmers who grew sugar cane and fruit were accompanied by their families. Coastal settlements sprang up.

Detail from Hazel Pride. *Cane Fire across the Railway Line, Redlynch.* 1960.

Shopkeepers were identities, like Mary Margaret Balocco, of Redlynch, the wife of Eddie and sister of Joe Chirio. She told me how, as a little girl, she and her family slept under a bullock dray at Port Douglas till her father found a place for them to live. They established a farm growing tropical fruit, especially pawpaws, for export south to Townsville and Brisbane by ship, about 1890. There was no refrigeration for the fruit and Mary believed that the agents did not give them a proper return in money, by saying that the fruit went bad.

In the early years of the twentieth century it was popular to go walking among the trees and the orchids and to look at the river and the rainforest. If you ever walk by the Barron River at Kamerunga, pause a moment to think about Nellie, a young woman who enjoyed taking the children there nearly one hundred years ago. She wrote to 'Mary', at North Hill, Forbes, in New South Wales on a 1920's photo-postcard of a man, lady and a dog with the caption 'Parks and gardens, Kamerunga.' now in the Mitchell Library, Sydney.

'Dear Mary,

> Just a line to let you know I am still alive. The children are all well and often talk about you and little Mary. Heather has been walking since she was ten months old she is not very big but terrible fat. She still has the breast. I think I will have a treat to take it from her she can ask me for it now. How are they all at home? I wrote but they never answered it about four months ago. I will write a long letter home I am not sure about the address.

Love Nellie'

The Barron River spreads outside its great mountainous gorge at Kamerunga, where a bridge takes traffic across. It once was a place for Bama ceremonies, hunting, and fishing on the sandy banks over which the annual floods rise dramatically. A deep swimming hole in the river was believed to have dangerous spirits that caught swimmers at Kamerunga.

Keeping records

I used to enjoy exploring the rainforest on the steep slopes there, and once I did First Aid with an ice pack on a lad stung by a stone fish.

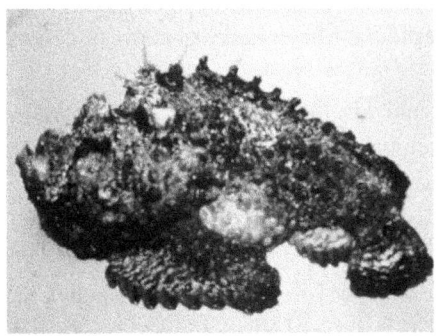

A stone fish

This Wet Season children's essay that I wrote was published in the *The Courier-Mail* in 1948.

Caught in Flood

We thought our Easter would be a very quiet one, but it turned out to be interesting. On Saturday night we went to the local pictures. The road to the theatre is over bridges which cross the one creek in different places, and this creek rises and falls very suddenly.

When we came to one bridge on our return, it was completely submerged by deep, swirling flood waters, so we went to try the higher cane bridge. We could not even reach a spot within half a mile of it. We returned to the other bridge and spent the night in the tiny sedan, waiting for the flood to recede. There were five of us, most uncomfortably cramped.

By dawn, the creek was still rising, so we were forced to leave the car in a safe spot and walk across a narrow railway bridge which extends for more than a quarter of a mile above low-lying cane fields, now floating in water. Had we fallen in, we would have been lucky to come out alive.

When we reached home, we all had a big breakfast, and went to bed to catch up on sleep. We were resting in the afternoon when mother saw a huge green snake in the lounge. After a search we found and killed it.

That night after tea I heard a terrified squawk in the fowl house. We all grabbed lanterns and found what we expected—an evil-looking brown snake, just finishing a chicken supper. After we had killed the writhing brute, mother skinned it. It has a pretty yellow belly with a pale chocolate back. So our Easter brought plenty of interest.

Fifty years ago in the North, people in newspapers thought in black and white fonts and smelt the hot metal on the linotype. Then, local editorial opportunities were sparse. Photo-block making was expensive, because it was sent away to Townsville or Brisbane by train or plane. Books were occasionally published in Sydney or Melbourne, or London; there was no television.

The Cairns Post, where I worked, was the daily newspaper that was locally owned. The offices had heavy manual typewriters, a teleprinter, seven telephone lines to Editorial, a reader who could take photos, and no computers. In quaint jargon, we 'checked', 'cut', 'pasted', 'subedited', 'ran' or 'spiked' our copy.

The Cairns Post

Today the foothills are full of fast developing suburbs but those foothills have had golden moments; prospectors dug at the Second Tunnel creek campsite. The Aboriginal camp at Darrella was moved to make way for an unsuccessful gold mine prospect, tunnelling into the hillside near the graves of Djabugay old people.

The history of the development of the Aboriginal settlement, with its Dammari stories, has good and bad memories for many of the Redlynch Bama, who buried their loved ones there.

A gold prospecting shaft at Darrella, 1996

Expressing Grief

The spontaneous expression of personal loss, the right to mourn openly, is a cultural norm of Aboriginal peoples. Open grief has not yet been incorporated by white society into their death protocols, but white society is learning. The Bama suspend all regular social events for death rituals, which maintain social bonding and cohesion of the tribes. The mourning of their tragedies was expressed traditionally in their women's soulful song and dance cycles.

Traditionally mummification was performed in the Dry season and burials were done in the Wet season. Sometimes there was later cremation or carrying the parcel of remains of a loved one. At Mona Mona Mission the ashes of a dead family member were, on occasion, ceremonially placed in the river. They also suppressed the use of a dead person's name or picture for some years to ease the pain of the relatives.

Four hundred Aboriginal men fought in World War I and 5,000 in World War II, but those who came back to Queensland had their wages sequestered (Hooper, 2008, p. 115). About 5,000 Europeans from Australia north of the Tropic of Capricorn died in the five wars between the outbreak of the Boer War and the end of the Vietnam engagement. In Australia, say from 1861 to 1930, as many as 10,000 Blacks were killed in skirmishes with the Europeans in North Queensland (Reynolds, 1982, p. 35, 201).

The silence of personal pain at the loss of the loved ones developed in the West as a reaction to the overload of sorrow caused by the two World Wars. Stoic survival in battlefront trenches and civilian devastation brought about a silence, like a granite crust. Indigenous and white men feel it more acutely than their women, who sometimes weep for them while they weep themselves.

Disallowing the outward face of private pain with the rule that men don't cry and women do has disastrous consequences in men's inner suffering. It often results in men's heavy drinking and domestic violence as their grief, rage and sorrow come out. It is so painful to watch.

CHAPTER 5
MONA MONA AND YARRABAH MISSIONS

The Federal government put looking after the natives into the hands of the churches. The churches made a social investment for faith, shouldering the moral obligations of the new nation and getting control over the Aboriginal peoples' bodies and souls. The destruction of the myth of the 'noble savage' in the face of threat by 'fearsome natives' was an ideological charter for social action, permitting emotional and physical violence. Some 7,000 Aboriginal people were forced into reserves by 1939 (Fitzgerald et al., 2009, p. 46).

There were some conscientious people among the pioneers when they came from the old country. The missionaries were often the only people who tried to prevent other Europeans from doing dreadful things to the Bama. Defying selectors, they set up safe havens on their territory to remove Aboriginal people from attack. Often it was the committed missionary who resisted culture change imposed by governments and landowners. The price was their ability to survive. For example, Rev John Brown Gribble died at Yarrabah at the age of forty-seven.

For over a century, then, the church and state have been more-or-less parents for Aboriginal young people struggling to do without their own parents due to government policy and colonial history. These institutions could give courage, inspiration, an hour's holiday now and then, or cause furious debate over reconciliation, native title, child abuse and recognition of fault in the ideology of past practices.

Removal from the family campsites, the centres of the Bama community and culture, to the missions, was a culture shock. As a result, the old Bama culture was virtually destroyed when the mission era began in 1913.

On the mission stations, the Bama people were gathered into larger communities with strangers from other tribes. In time, some of the Bama went from the missions to jobs on farms; others were given rations by the government so they would not raid the settlers. However, if an Aboriginal person spat at a missionary (or a Member of Parliament) or urinated on an altar (it happened) they were asking for a flogging, pack-drill or to be chained up.

> 'When Rev. J. B. Gribble had been at Warangesda Mission station on the Murrumbidgee River, NSW, he had reported on the "vicious habits" of the Whites. In one Aboriginal camp he had visited there were eleven women and girls abandoned (because of syphilis), with scarcely a rag to cover them, and not a morsel of food in their possession' (Cannon, 1973, p. 20).

In 1897, John Gribble established Yarrabah as a settlement for Aboriginal people across the Trinity Bay Inlet from the city of Cairns. 'Yarrabah' is the name of its hill, taken from 'jun jun yarra, the fish hawk who fell after constant circling the fishes' (Bottoms, 1990, p. 233). It was a Church of England Mission. John's son Ernest ran Yarrabah till 1909. Two hundred full-blood Bama were captured and confined there as a way of dealing with the 'native' problem.

A century ago, with their culture in disarray as white settlers moved into the countryside, alcohol and opium addiction were adopted by Murris. An effort was made to stop its destructive effects. The Aboriginals Protection and Restriction of the Sale of Opium Act of 1897 imposed oppressive authority over the tribes. It affected their right to marry, to live with their children and to work. The Act also prevented Aboriginal people from controlling their wages, their money, their property, and to travel, to use the law, to receive mail, and to practise their religion. It allowed them to be jailed or flogged (Bottoms, 1995, pp. 6, 9).

Patsy Pride and Zelda Appleby with aboriginal children at Yarrabah in 1953. Photo by Berkely Cook.

The Aboriginal Preservation and Protection Act 1939–1965, which replaced the 1897 Act, maintained and strengthened many of its original principles and practices (Haebich, 2000, p. 171). The Queensland government has calculated that 2,302 children were taken from parents to missions and settlements (Hooper, 2008, p. 57).

The tragedy is that on all the missions and settlements Aboriginal people suffered deprivation of basic amenities, with official attitudes steeped in nineteenth century environmentalism (Kidd, 1997, p. 97).

By 1960, Yarrabah was a government-run station for Aboriginal peoples from different areas. Today, instead of being a boat trip away from town it is connected by a sealed road through a developing part of Cairns city.

'Bringing children up takes years, every day. Seeing your parents a couple of times a week and scrubbing floors in a mission did not teach them about coping with AIDS, or bush food health eating' was said to me recently by a Bama woman who was working with the casualties on a daily basis.

Schoolchildren at lunchtime in the playground at Yarrabah, 1967

Mona Mona and Yarrabah

The Seventh Day Adventist Mission was established in 1913, fifteen kilometres north-west of Kuranda on Flaggy Creek. The mission was called 'Mona Mona', from the Djabugay word, meaning 'crooked' which referred to the course of the creek.

In two years, 103 Bama had been put at the Mission. In 1915, the police rounded up fifty-six people at Speewah to take them to Mona Mona because the Bama runner had not got through in time to warn the Aboriginal adults. Mixed race children were reared in dormitories without their parents, their language or their culture. The scheme lasted till 1962 (Bottoms, 1995, p. 7).

Mona Mona Mission was the home to half caste Aboriginal people. Kuranda businessmen lobbied against the removal of the local Aboriginal people to Mona Mona Mission, declaring them to be 'a wonderful little tribe of niggers.' Furthermore, they were very interesting to tourists and would probably be of great commercial value to the mission (Kidd, 2000, p. 71–72).

The Mona Mona Mission land is 1,610 hectares big. The residents are currently camping in leaky dwellings without facilities and infrastructure. They want tenure over the land to make plans, while the State Government has offered them trusteeship over part of it. Federal funding of $2.6 million put aside in 1995 has now been dispersed, and little progress has been made in negotiations (Law, 2009, pp.18-23).

NQ in Black and White

Steven and Mona Fagan

CHAPTER 6

STEVEN AND MONA FAGAN

A LIFE STORY

Mrs Mona Fagan was a charismatic old lady with a vision to change the myth of Aboriginal sovereignty into reality. I recorded her story before she died (Fagan, 1996). Mona and Stephen really wanted their story, their part of the Bama Storywater, to be heard and accepted.

Their daughter Muriel and a granddaughter gave their permission for me to transcribe Mona and Stephen's story. The Fagan's children also helped Kanakas and Torres Strait Islanders be part of the North Queensland community.

Mona spoke for her generation, a positive example of what the Mona Mona Mission could to do with mixed-descent children. The Seventh Day Adventists had established and run this Mission.

Mrs Fagan was born at Crystal Cascades, near Redlynch, in 1914 and didn't remember her birth mother much or know who her white father was, because she was taken to the mission when she was two years old.

Mona had a photograph of a man, a very traditional full-blood Aboriginal, whom she considered as her 'father'. She had too many mothers. She said, 'I couldn't tell you how many'. She said that she only came back to Redlynch a few times before she was married.

Mona was initiated, like her Aboriginal father and mother, with cicatrice on the chest, three scars for bravery. She didn't talk about it for fear of offending the spirits. The initiation ceremony was held at Oak Forest (named after the indigenous she-oak trees) near Kuranda.

Mothers and grandmothers were ritually cut on the chest, at about fourteen. The initiation taught bravery and scars are records of heroic deeds done for honour in the tribe.

When she was twenty-four, Mona married Steven Fagan, a young man who had been the first baby born on Mona Mona Mission. He had spent some years in the Mareeba district in the Atherton Tablelands timber industry as a lorry driver. Mona worked at the mission school, teaching, after she was married. They had their first child a year after their church wedding. They had three sons and three daughters.

The mission had a stove and a big ant-bed oven in which bread was made every Monday and Friday, when the children all had a big helping. Shaping it round, Mona showed the form of the oven, which was made from wet ant-bed with thick walls over wire and clay. The workers used to collect the ant-bed in the bullock wagon or a spring cart.

'You can still do it today, and the bread tastes better', she reminisced and in her mind smelled the yeast as the loaves rose and were taken out when the little tin door was opened.

A young Yirrganydji leader who looked like a real Indian (from India), or a Tasmanian, came to visit Mona Mona when he was about eighteen. He had got out of the Redlynch tribe and stayed fourteen days. His own tribe saw him as 'King Billy', calling him 'Jagga'.

'In our humpies we moved him around this way and that way because he was scared; we were sad when he went away,' said Mona.

Jeanette Singleton, a Yirrganydji lady, had a splendid photo of him and told many stories about his activities.

Steven and Mona wanted to be decent parents, whom sons could see as good models and with whom girls can feel secure as they become women. As children Steven and Mona hadn't had that with their own biological fathers; they were taken to be brought up at the mission. They had bonded with senior Bama as parents in the mission community. The adults were accommodated in native huts while the children were reared in dormitories.

As the mission struggled with debts, their endowment money from the government was kept as a necessary resource. Steven and Mona were told that if they kept asking what money was in their names, they would be sent to Palm Island, a medical 'prison'. It was not until Steven was forty that he learned to read and write. Remembering the past, Steven burst out with a sense of grievance, in contrast to his normally quiet and dignified manner.

After two years of applications, Steven's wages were finally paid to him directly. Sometimes, the fortnightly endowment was not paid and they did not know how much money they would have for a couple of months. Steven lived to be a great old man into his eighties, dying in January 2009.

Current research shows that the Queensland government recognised that compensation should be paid to the Aboriginal workers who had been underpaid. In February 2003, compensation payments began. Eligible applicants born on or before 31 December 1951 were entitled to $4,000. Apparently some Aboriginal people were ambivalent about accepting the payment because it did not 'represent the amount of the stolen wages' (Fitzgerald et al., 2009, p. 255).

Stephen and Mona's home at Oak Forest

CHAPTER 7
THE MISSION YEARS

On the Cape York Peninsula, the customs and beliefs of the hunter-gatherers prevailed for centuries. European missionaries brought their religious values and technology when they came to claim land as settlers, so a culture clash was inevitable. Some Europeans were willing to learn from the Aboriginal people and work alongside them. Mrs Geraldine Mackenzie's 1981 book *Aurukun Diary: Forty Years with the Aborigines* provides a sympathetic record of the clash between cultures and the efforts made by black and white people to understand one another.

A century ago Australian churches, with government approval, made a social investment in the care of Aboriginal people. However, the benign handing out of food for every meal and communal feeding of the old and young had an underside: it kept people like children. Both children and parents considered the transfer of children from camps into missions as child theft with far-reaching consequences: lost birth families, lost culture, lost habitation and lost Native Title claims.

Human beings are made subjects (and objects) by power and knowledge. Discourses of life, labour and language are turned into disciplines. Ideology and political hegemony in any society depends on the ability to control the material context of personal and social experience (Harvey, 1989, pp. 214, 227).

If you simply break down a cultural role, however good or bad it might have been and offer nothing in its place, you demoralise people. In a life without kin bonding there are little loves and cruelties and large mental repercussions for lonely kids and parents, families and even nations, replete with domestic breakdowns, betrayals, drug dependence, failure and disillusionment.

Dr Eric Mjoberg was a Swedish anthropologist and collector of insects, animals and plants. He observed the listless compliance of the Yarrabah Mission population near Cairns and the struggles of the missionaries in 1913. He felt these were largely due to being located in the wrong place, such as a disease-infected swamp, with no access to fresh vegetables and fruit. Their belief that they and their children had been captured, horrified the Murris (Mjoberg, 1918/1986, p. 236).

The animist beliefs of Australian Aboriginal tribes intrigued him. Dr Mjoberg visited North Queensland in 1913 and lived among the Bama for some time, describing the grass huts and way of life of those at Kuranda. He wrote 'they constitute a curiosity in the eyes of tourists, who previously only knew this race in theory. They come into their camp and for a trifling price buy a lot of curiosities like boomerangs, rattan baskets, etc.' (Mjoberg, 1918/1986, pp. 62–74).

The full English translation of Mjoberg's detailed accounts was not published at the time because of its contentiousness. There is now a copy in the Oxley Library, Brisbane. His collection of over 100,000 artefacts was distributed among specialist halls of learning and is catalogued at the Australian Institute of Aboriginal and Torres Strait Islander Studies (AIATSIS), Canberra. His defence of Indigenous rights and identity was, when seen from a Eurocentric point of view, embarrassingly eccentric.

'During my first expedition [to the Kimberleys] I had already had occasion to observe missionaries of different persuasions and communions perform their responsible task, namely to take charge of the primitive Australian aborigines, who had greatly degenerated thanks to civilisation. This aspect of the state's functions is in the main performed fairly secretly (in considerable obscurity) and without the necessarily degree of control and due understanding. Those who are really informed on the matter and in a position to judge the situation have realised that the whole "native question" has been bungled and turned into a party matter, and do not dare to speak their mind plainly and press for improvement. As a result this especially important question has become a matter of laisser-aller and also one of the most unfortunate aspects of the (Australian) administration, which is very capable in many other respects' (Mjoberg, 1918/1986, pp. 31–259, 378).

Mjoberg was outraged at the intrusion of white culture into sites like Mornington Island and tried in vain to prevent such interventions by writing to learned societies and the Swedish consul in Sydney. There were interstate rivalries and no-one dared to break with the missionaries and their protectors. Two Queensland Protectors of Aborigines resigned in protest (Mjoberg, 1918/1986, p. 372). The missionaries provoked the blacks on Mornington Island until they chopped off the mission superintendent's head with a tomahawk (Mjoberg, 1918/1986, p. 378). The newcomers had condemned nakedness, and ceremonies and told the Aboriginal men and women whom they should marry (Mjoberg, 1918/1986).

Aurukun Aboriginal people claimed their reserve land as their own in a legal battle, which they lost, to prevent the development of a large bauxite mining port (Fitzgerald et al., 2009, p. 168).

Now the people of Mornington Island and Aurukun elect Shire Councils after struggles for management between the people, the Commonwealth of Australia and the State of Queensland.

In *From Hunting to Drinking*, anthropologist David McKnight summed up the social emergency in these settlements:

> 'Tension and aggression dominate all social intercourse. Suicide and the homicide rate on Mornington Island and Doomadgee is twenty-five times that of any other settlement in Queensland' (McKnight, 2008, p. 2).

CHAPTER 8
SELF-DESTRUCTION

In despair away from his European cultural roots, the first superintendent of the Palm Island mission in the 1920s, Robert Curry, had been a cruel, violent man. His hatred of the local doctor intensified when his wife died in childbirth. He lost control in a rampaging outburst of destructive entitlement and so was shot. The old Indigenous people sang 'this country made him die; the place he did not belong to' (Hooper, 2008, p. 82).

The Bama see themselves as inseparable from the landscape, their Bulmba; it is their identity and the meaning of life. They too may feel lost if relocated by civil officials to Palm Island. Problems amongst the people were often the results of members of a number of races and tribes being made to live closely to one another and being confined to one location. Their loss of homeland and tribal group showed in the Bama people's behaviour as aimlessness, boredom and irresponsibility.

The evil spirit of depression is contagious, with its sense of closed futility in an unfriendly land. In the community it prompts self-destruction as the folk try to cope with dark secrets and ritual grief at funerals, like the one at Yarrabah for a fourteen-year-old girl who took her own life in 2001. A fourteen-month-old baby was raped and murdered there in January 2007. Both the mother and the killer were from Palm Island (Hooper, 2008, p. 244).

Indigenous life expectancy was fifteen years to twenty years lower than that of other Queenslanders. Indigenous youths were over-represented in crime statistics, and, most disturbingly, the suicide rate for young Queensland Indigenous males was three-

and-a-half times that of all young Queensland males (Fitzgerald, 2009, p. 197).

Loss of purpose, sometimes called anomie, may have caused the deaths of all the Djabugay men whom I photographed demonstrating a crocodile corroboree at Yarrabah in September 1967. Except for Tommy Hall they were fairly young. 'There are no youths here carrying on the traditions', they told me sadly. Or could children learn them?

Getting ready to dance at Yarrabah 1967

Second from left: Dudley Bulmer (Cooktown)
Third from left: Wilfred Harris (Gungganydji)
Forth from left: Frank Bulmer
Seated: Tommy Hall

Self-destruction

Kelvin Hill learned to throw a boomerang at Redlynch. He lived with Aboriginal people for twenty years as a white medical worker with his wife, Matron Helen Hill. For some of that time they were at Yarrabah Mission, where he was adopted by the expatriate Djabugay. But he was upset by their self-destructiveness. He told me that when Aboriginal people were arrested for habitual drunkenness and put in police cells, they suffered awful withdrawal symptoms later. That was why they hanged themselves sometimes.

> 'This is the deadliest society in the world. Transgression of the law means death and, forced together, they have to break taboos. I couldn't stand it to see them killing themselves with drink or, sometimes, each other.' (Hill, 1993)

Even with his deep insight he could not escape the atmosphere of doom about them all. I could not go to help him and his wife then. Kelvin himself went flying one more time above his beloved mountain in 1995. His plane crashed, and he died there.

Away south in Melbourne's St Kilda, a Cairns Murri was one of the 'parkies', sleeping out near the Catani Gardens toilet which was a useful windbreak and had Koori artwork on it – until the 'Grand Prix' park clean-up some years ago. He went down to the trees of the foreshore at Brighton and hanged himself. The police sent his body back north.

Kelvin Hill at Tully in 1993

Self-destruction

At the 1997 National Enquiry on separated children, Professor Ernest Hunter said

> 'I believe that violence to significant others and self-harm are related and represent the enactment, at the centre of Aboriginal societies, that is, within the family, of the consequences of the protracted and damaging intrusion into family life that accompanied and followed colonisation' (Hunter, 1997, p. 11).

Dr Nick Kowalenko's studies agree with Professor Hunter. Here is an excerpt from the same enquiry:

> 'Separated children want later to be good parents themselves, but in some way disruption and loss have been built into them as a way of defending against the need that their children may have for them in a consistent and ongoing fashion. They might then become afraid of the dependency of the children, or they might become afraid of the needs of their children and they might not be as ready to ensure that all the things that maintain trust and continuity with the care of their children can be sustained.' (Kowalenko, 1997, p. 227).

For Murris, the tradition of telling stories round the warming fire at night, as it glowed from embers at the entrance to the gunya, has changed. It might have become a fire of sticks on a sheet of galvanised iron indoors or in a caravan, with all its risks. Feeling trapped inside four walls, Aboriginal people are struggling to keep in touch with the diminishing traditional way of life. It has been more important to maintain the evening fires, a tradition they can keep up, than to worry about the permanent house fabric.

The social engineering brings toxic stress as lives are changed irreversibly; the Murris have nothing to steady themselves with; they are not in control of their lives. A 1992 Government national survey of ATSIC housing in the Cairns district (excluding Yarrabah) found much overcrowding and fifty-two per cent of houses needed repair. Half of the sixteen per cent of Indigenous people had changed their address since 1986 according to the National Bureau of Statistics census of 1994. The median age of twenty was well below the Queensland median age of thirty-two years. In 1994 there were 1,783 Aboriginal people at Yarrabah, and 733 at Mareeba, some of whom were Djabugay.

Current living conditions are similarly revealing, supporting Aboriginal grievances. Unfortunately, Indigenous youths arrested for offences such as theft, often are taken into detention if they are homeless.

The late Mick Miller, the former North Queensland Land Council Chairman, struggled with these social crises and with his own diabetes. We were walking together when he shook his head about the way things were.

> 'Depression hangs over most Aboriginal men's lives. They need meaningful roles and work. Opportunities for their children would improve men's outlook. Boys can have improved mental health from early adolescence onward. Some of our people are dying because of shattered ideals of honour and courage. If they are surrounded by despair, apathy and rage, will they be able to solve their own problems?'

Asking the right questions can be as hard as getting opposing ideas together. The words of Peter Yu, a former Kimberley Land Council executive, are enlightening.

'It is internalised oppression; that's what it is. We know it is in our own families, with men who have been through institutions. Most women have this experience. It's horrible, terrible. The systems in place at the moment aren't able to deal with it. The survival of the Indigenous people is at stake' (Yu, 2001).

Surely, demanding adult behaviour while treating adults as children is psychological game playing; casting a spell over them. It is an old technique of subtle sorcery with power. A psychologist, Dr Richard Trahair, explained what has happened with European black magic:

'First infantilise the group. Make them babies by taking away responsibility. Then expose them to your anxieties so they carry them around. Punish them for their wickedness by removing them from social structures which build identity, like the tribe, the family, the land. Without them they are completely lost, but the rules say it's alright.

'Invading forces cast a spell over the tribes they conquer without knowing they are doing it. The victors are filled with the euphoria of winning territory, of finding their own place. Because the negative enchantment is secret they themselves never learn. The invaders make heroes and heroines from 'stolen' or abandoned children, like the prophets in exile. (Moses just wanted his mother back; Oedipus just wanted his land back; Ned Kelly wanted to get his mother out of gaol.) They were made great by overcoming adversity. Aboriginal people have had to become political heroes and heroines to get back what was taken away from them. For them this has been legalised as civil rights and land rights' (Trahair, 1994).

In her book, *The Tall Man,* Chloe Hooper (2008) writes of the drama in the tropical humidity at the trial of Senior Sergeant Christopher Hurley. He was acquitted of causing the death in custody of Mulrunji Doomadgee in a Palm Island gaol on 19 November 2004. The court heard that Mulrunji had been taken from his home at Doomadgee in the Gulf Country and been confined to life on the island where drunkenness and violence is endemic.

He was drunk and singing as he walked along one morning. He passed the policeman in his van and swore at him. Incensed, Hurley arrested him and thrust him into his van. A few minutes later Mulrunji struck the policeman on the jaw and Hurley punched him in the ribs. As they moved into the police station they fell into the doorway. There was a struggle, a nasty turn of events. Time seemed to bend and stretch as the moments ticked by and life ebbed away. An hour later, Mulrunji was dead with his liver split almost in two as he lay on the cell floor.

A riot occurred on Palm Island; the police station was burned down, in the release of all the rage of those fatherless generations where a history of deprivation was omnipresent (Hooper, 2008, p. 70).

The following protracted enquiry, inquest and trial of Hurley is a landmark case of another Aboriginal death in custody. For the first time, a policeman admitted he had caused a death in custody and had gone before a jury. A sad consequence of Doomadgee's death was the suicide of his seventeen year old son Eric after the funeral, in his feelings of grief and hopelessness.

Think of Sydney Parkinson, the 1770 explorer from HMS *Endeavour*, and Mulrunji Doomadgee in 2004, the Palm Island resident. In this mental picture, two brave men express their nation's ideals but one will die. Sydney Parkinson died in 1770, but in 2004 it is the Australian Aboriginal man who would die.

The Crime and Misconduct Commission Officers condemned the trial as seriously flawed and full of police cover-ups in their review released on 17 June 2010. The death, riots and ruin that followed confirm this opinion.

The deplorable situation for Aboriginal people prompted the Commonwealth Housing and Infrastructure Needs Survey (CHINS) in 2006. Indigenous Housing Organisations in the Commonwealth managed 21,854 permanent dwellings by 2006, thirty-four per cent requiring major repairs or replacement. Four per cent were temporary dwellings. The average weekly rent was $48.

Bore water was the source of drinking water for fifty-eight per cent of communities; some had water carted in. Only nine communities had no organised water supply. Some communities chlorinated their drinking water; others did not.

The main sources of electricity are community diesel generators, grid supply then solar power. Interruptions often occur.

Fifty three per cent of residents reported public access to a telephone; eleven per cent had access to the Internet, mostly in the Council office. Most received television and radio broadcasts. Queensland had sixty-three communities without public telephones.

More communities have secondary schools up to Year 12 but eleven per cent of Queensland settlements are twenty-five kilometres or more from a primary school.

Indigenous male and female trained workers help with issues of mental and sexual health, alcohol, ear and eye health, diabetes, hospital education and liaison with doctors. Hospitals could be more than one hundred kilometres away from Indigenous communities.

Some flush toilets with a sewage treatment plant were being put in, but septic tanks with leach drains were the most common type of sewerage system, with pit toilets in smaller communities. There were fewer rubbish collections in isolated communities than in city suburbs.

CHAPTER 9

TAKEAWAY CHILDREN

'People who live with toxic shame feel fundamentally disgraced, intrinsically worthless, and profoundly humiliated in their own skin, just for being themselves' wrote Professor James Garbarino of Cornell University in the United States of America.

Professor Garbarino specialises in what causes violence in children, on child abuse and neglect, on their traumatic background, and what to do about bullying at school. He is an advisor to many organisations, including the National Black Child Development Institute. He has found that because of the overwhelming effects of the trauma, individuals come to expect bad things to happen and even re-enact and replicate their bad experiences by inviting negative reactions (Garbarino et al., 1998).

Mental health doctors report that children separated from their parents were less likely to be in a stable relationship with a partner, twice as likely to admit having been arrested and convicted, three times as likely to have been in jail, twice as likely to report drug use and more likely to die in custody.

> 'Perhaps because it is such an overwhelming problem, people have distanced themselves from it' (Raphael, 1996).

In Australia, Cape York's Aboriginal towns and settlements have been seriously affected. Social dysfunction among Queensland's Indigenous population was most severe in geographically remote Aboriginal settlements. Unemployment, poverty and lack of outside scrutiny, which comes with living in remote areas, led to severe problems with child sex abuse, alcoholism, and violence and school truancy.

Justice Tony Fitzgerald was commissioned in July 2001 to develop a management plan for alcohol and drug abuse which was destroying the Indigenous communities. His report highlighted the serious impact that alcohol addiction had in creating or accentuating poverty, health problems and violence, particularly against women. There was a high incidence of children born with brain damage through foetal alcohol syndrome. The government encouraged Alcohol Management Plans which allowed for the declaration of 'dry zones' backed up by serious police enforcement (Fitzgerald et al., 2009, p. 254).

Along with the worrisome use of alcohol and cigarettes by teenagers and even younger children, are bigger worries: marijuana, other drugs and AIDS. Young people try to deal with the unfamiliar and intense emotions of their adolescence. These elements, along with sleep difficulties, extra arousal, aggressive behaviour and depression reflect the trauma and grief. These are some reasons why youth suicide is at high levels.

Takeaway children who were in institutions frequently did not receive much affection. The main concerns of their carers were that the children 'conformed' and were compliant, rather than were shown love. Young people thus might feel guilty and overwhelmed. To tell their story is very stressful. While their search for lost mothers, fathers and relatives may have thrilling results, separated children can feel exhausted by sad personal memories and confused about identity. What is missing is talk and laughter round the family fire at home. Instead, many feel they do not have enough resources themselves to deal with the traumas of the past.

Adult commitment helps fulfil an individual but it can bring a re-enactment of separation anxiety in new relationships.

There may be brothers and sisters unseen, taken away. Perhaps there are bad secrets, but who wants to hear about 'kid frigging' as one of the 'kids' confided to me? He was a shattered young man. Nobody wants to take the responsibility before it is too late. Who is to ask abusive staff or weekend 'hosts' for compensation or apology for an unbearably painful experience, for endless nightmares or wetting the bed?

Claims about assaults of children at school involve dragging up those painful and bad feelings. Victims have found no faith in church school hierarchies in Queensland. These young people struggle to get real legal advice so delay production of statutory declarations against the perpetrator. Instead they may be treated as enemies in the fight against insurers within statutory time limits at the risk of enormous legal costs to the victims as revealed by the Project Access Survey by the Queensland Department of Justice (Carrick, 2009).

Mentally traumatised Aboriginal adults may find their relationships tarnished by fear of their children being taken away, fear of psychologists and psychiatrists, and fear of government laws on sterilisation, euthanasia, domestic violence and alcoholism. Fear of tribal law and white legislation can keep them in unhappy marriages or out of happy ones.

Removed children lost contact with distinct Aboriginal family ties and traditions surrounding child birth and parenting. Some members of the 'Stolen Generation' have trouble expressing affection and attaching to their own children. Young Aboriginal men and women are unable to deal with other mentally ill Aboriginal people as this role was historically the role of tribal elders. Their strict cultural upbringing gave the elders patience and understanding when helping mentally ill people. The elders ensured there were clevermen, like the wayan, to speak to the spirit making the Aboriginal person mentally ill.

For Dr Mick Dodson, 2009 Australian of the Year and lawyer, the frontiers are everywhere. In 1997, he made a most moving plea for the hurt in the hearts of mothers, not only birth mothers but foster mothers.

> 'We have not heard about those mothers of the stolen children. How could they come to us and talk about their pain? To the parents who loved and fostered these children I cannot imagine the wretched pain they must be going through because they believed they were doing the right thing. There were too few to be noticed. I express my sorrow on the pain they are enduring.'

Foster carers work in a time between the institution days, when washing walls and floors for girls and farm labour for boys was enough training, and the new global economy. Now, other kids at school come from families that use mobile telephones, television, CDs, computers, the Internet, DVDs and motor cars. Aboriginal kindred carers may get less help than foster parents. Mental and physical child abuse occurs sometimes in these homes, and the vulnerable may carry their scars for life.

CHAPTER 10

MEDICINE MEN

The health of our minds and our bodies is in both our hands; black and white acting together. This chapter can only give a few examples of the great issues in the sociology of health in Australia's North, whose seriousness always appears to be slipping off our agenda. The health problems are the results of poor food, drink, overcrowding, disease and violence, as well as substance abuse and its destructive effects on the patient, the family and the entire community.

Into the humid medical climate in Cairns, on Christmas Day 1963, came Mrs Gladys O' Shane, the Bama wife of a colourful Irish wharf labourer, Paddy 'Tiger' O' Shane. She was mother of Pat and Terry and grandmother of Tjandamurra. Gladys was an intelligent, vigorous, charming woman in the prime of her life. The family sat down to roast chicken for dinner.

On her first mouthful, Gladys unfortunately got a bone stuck in her throat, causing serious pain and swelling. The family quickly made their way to the Cairns Base Hospital, where after a routine examination she was sent home. All the doctors were at the staff Christmas dinner. Her daughter Pat watched the purple face and the swelling with alarm and took her back. An operation was in due course performed, but in haste the vagus nerve and its vital functions were damaged in the removal of the bone. Gladys lapsed into a coma and she died the following year.

The tragedy traumatised the family and they became very active in legal issues. The hospital was embarrassed. The Murris, in shock, at once suspected sorcery. In a case such as this malevolent spirits were blamed, probably to the relief of the hospital Board.

Many Murris are often afraid of European medical methods. They use their own healing solutions when confronted by diseases they recognise. When dealing with whitefella diseases they have a problem if they do not trust the doctor.

New drug treatments have brought reliable changes, especially to Murri patients in outlying country areas, who can come to the city for treatment sometimes. However, if Murris are afflicted by schizophrenia for instance, which they see as whitefella illness, they look for a whitefella cure. Naturally, it will only be able to work if the Murri takes the medication as directed, otherwise they will be back where they started.

The Bama can rightly blame woes on introduced diseases such as tuberculosis and venereal disease and lifestyles with alcohol, petrol sniffing, high sugar foods and drugs. Meanwhile, the Gadja blame Bama for lack of control of alcohol and smoking and improper use of medicines and medical help.

Adjunct Professor Ian Ring, when Head of the Discipline of Public Health and Tropical Medicine at James Cook University in Townsville, said that experience shows the need to improve Indigenous housing, water, land, education, economic development and early medical treatment with its own skilled Murri professionals.

> 'A poor Whitefella diet is producing an epidemic of diabetes, especially in remote communities on the mainland and in the Torres Strait. It is hard to get acceptance of the need for high fibre foods and fresh vegetables to lower the intake of sugar

and fats. This would reduce the nerve damage to people's feet and reduce amputations' (Ring, 2001).

The fight against dengue fever and other insect-borne diseases, by draining waste water holes and stagnant sewage, has made the tropics a much healthier place. Yet Aboriginal young adult mortality rates are the highest in the world outside war zones. Furthermore, perinatal and child mortality rates are around three times those of other Australians and maternal mortality rates are more than twice those for other Australian women. Aboriginal women also have much higher rates of death from cervical cancer.

The National Centre for Aboriginal and Torres Strait Islander Statistics has been working to improve statistics gathering. However, each Australian State has different questions about Aboriginality on their birth and death forms, which makes analysis difficult. For instance, Queensland death statistics for Murris only came in during 1997 (Scott, 2002). A national long term health study of women, based on health insurance, had fewer numbers of Indigenous participants in North Australia. Statistics on perinatal deaths go back to 1994 but they do not account for children born to Indigenous fathers but non-Indigenous mothers.

But it is in the fraught area of resource management of State Government and Federal funding that health care may take second place to sovereignty over land utilisation. This fearsome struggle is documented by Rosalind Kidd (2000) in her book *The way we civilise*. Murris were moved from their homelands. However, where groups of people are thrown together from different tribes and regions, communalism will just intensify the tensions between competing loyalties, Skin groups and resources.

These stresses were observed by Kelvin Hill, who assisted his wife Helen. She was the matron in the medical clinic at Yarrabah, and previously at Aurukun. Kelvin listened to Bama stories and tape recorded them. He told me that to treat a person with a fractured pelvis, for example, the Bama patient would be positioned in a depression in a sandy spot and rested until the injury recovered. It was like being in bed.

Bama and Gadja medical ways are different. The Maladambun is the sorcerer. He knows there is more than up, down, through and when; that trouble has an evil stench. The smells and fluids of the body may seep out effortlessly like gravity, under stress. They are signs.

'I believe in the Lightning String', says a patient. 'They throw it after (victims) with sorcery for good or ill. I had a pain in my shoulder and chest that wouldn't go away. The doctor could not find it. I went to the medicine man.' His invisible lightning sends a wavelength that reaches into the depths of the unconscious.

When a man or a woman believes they have been 'sung' by sorcery, they go to the witch doctor. A practitioner interpreting a fourth dimension, he can see the paranormal with the power of charm and chant and his mesmerising little branch. He wipes his hands over the sweat from his armpits, full of its mysterious magic, and then transposes it over his entranced patient to do away with the curse of the Lightning String. A pinched furrow on the brow relaxes; he chants to defeat the evil spirit. It is as if the earth's magnetism in space and time is at the will of the Maladambun, who alone sings, and who may produce a bloody pebble as the cause of the trouble.

Triumphing in his theatre, the sorcerer can chant a death wish, purri purri, on an enemy, over part of the victim's body, such as hair or sweat, which is cursed and buried. The victim may be painted on a rock wall. He is made aware of his fate by signs or gossip; death is inevitable.

Now on the other hand, consider what my plastic surgeon Mr W. Gilbert, said as the needle went in, to distract me from the pain of my tropical legacy: cutting out skin cancers and stitching up my damaged legs. He probably saved my life in 1994, seeing that I have white skin.

'Remember Harold Blair, the Aboriginal opera singer? He came from Childers. I have a picture of him. Aboriginal skin colour gives the Aborigines protection against ultraviolet radiation which causes skin cancer, although they can get it on the soles of their feet. Mixed-race people have a safer time in the sun. How does one see the sun-safe genes on a chromosome? Just take down its genes and have a look! However pigmented races have an increased tendency towards the formation of keloid scars. These accentuated scars, usually bright red, are seen as appropriate signifiers. Secondary healing of the exposed lower dermis or skin underneath makes keloid scars more common. Drawing wounds and gashes together promotes less scarring.'

He finished stitching. Then he smiled and said 'From now on you wear slacks and hats!'

CHAPTER 11
CAPTURED IN PICTURES

Mental pictures in stories, songs and art are the Murris' 'photo albums'; their rock art galleries are their Titles Office, encyclopaedias and cathedrals, said Pamela, my Bama guide. In their painting style, Murris look down as hunters do, whereas the Gadja look forward.

The Inside Storywaters contained in the paintings and engravings are accessible to initiates who will respect them.

The Storywaters are ancestral morality tales. Each tale focuses on a specific place and explains the origins of landforms, cultural practices and world view. The Bama do not tell the Inside Storywaters to people who are not initiated in their community. The versions of the stories they tell others are the Outside Storywaters. These are the stories found in tourist shops.

The Indigenous sense of beauty, status and identity is also expressed in body art, with painted wave forms, lines and in scars. Cicatrices (scars), signify affection, or bravery in initiation for manhood and womanhood. Accentuated scars are caused by exposing the lower skin, with mud put in for 'designer' scars. Elders like Mona Fagan were initiated with this cicatrice and privileged 'Inside Stories'; she had the right to speak with authority on tribal business.

Parkinson's Endeavour River drawing of the wayan working his spell (see Chapter 1) shows the man's will to negotiate peace with strength as he holds his symbolic branch of leaves with his six-fingered hand. Such a hand is proof of a special gift belonging to a witchdoctor. His secret of having six fingers has remained quietly waiting between the pages, carefully recorded. The drawing was reproduced by Bernard Smith (1992, plate 97) in his book. Professor Smith was astonished when I showed him the six fingers. 'Oh,' he exclaimed. 'But stay with it, for you see it there for yourself.'

The powerful spell of sexdigitaly (having six fingers or toes) may have to be believed to be seen. Greater hand grip was admired. Some historians state that Anne Boleyn, mother of Queen Elizabeth the First, had six fingers. The gods of Easter Island had six fingers (See Appendix 5).

The Bama say that many sorcery secrets have been sung into the rock galleries. At Laura, in the rock paintings not far from Split Rock, there is depicted a man with an extra finger on each hand, next to the giant male and female fertility figures and boomerang. In south-eastern Cape York six fingers are shown on one hand twice and on both hands four times (Bullen, 1987, Table 15a). Hand stencils are also common identifiers in the cave paintings. Paintings indicate ownership.

Hand stencils are made by people blowing liquid clay on to a hand placed on the rock face. When the hand is taken away from the rock, it leaves a shape in the form of a hand and traces of genetic material. Unlike a clan marker, the style of this personal gesture expresses identity, like a burial memorial declares the soul of a dead person. A totem design says who died and who is to see and to know this.

The code of meanings of the geometric symbols in Bama artwork is carefully taught so that with this knowledge one can make further connections or restrict its context to those who are allowed to know it.

These graphic icons over the centuries show us a clear system of power relationships with the law and with supernatural forces. The Kuku Djungan people of south east Cape York, 150 kilometres from Laura, used powerful ceremonial rock art in a large cave at Ngarrabullgan. Young children's hand stencils illustrate 'this is your place where you were born'.

The cave is the women's birthplace site, with rock wall paintings of dancing figures. Fireplace charcoal in the cave has been radio-carbon dated at over 4,000 years. 'Ngarrabullgan' means 'the lady with the white hair'. It is the Bama name for Mt Mulligan, where a coal mine disaster in 1932 killed over one hundred and thirty people.

A male ceremonial cave with instructive rock art in mud, red ochre and white clay is also located in the ancient sandstone. The yellow stone in the area is from lake sediments, containing ammonites from salty seas. As Laura is located inland the fossils indicate that the seas rose as the climate warmed and the Ice Age melted, changing the location of the coast line.

Identity, ceremony, tribal rites and the Rainbow Serpent's power over nature are all manifest in the cave galleries at Bare Hill, near Mareeba. They are surrounded by later rock art traditions which were not protected by the dense rainforest.

Photographs taken in November 1955 are held by the Melbourne Museum. One caption reads:

> 'George Kidner, Negrito Aborigine, with his wife and child at Mona Mona Mission. George comes from Millaa Millaa. Sometimes works for Ken Atkinson on his station south from Ravenshoe, Atherton Tableland.'

A photo of Robbie Major has the caption:

> 'Negrito aborigine from Millaa Millaa with his foreman at the Tully Falls construction September 1955'.

This photograph was meant to show differences in stature, but it also shows a caring paternal attitude of the foreman.

The Melbourne Museum also holds over four hundred Aboriginal artefacts of the North Queensland region, including many painted shields and woven baskets. Melbourne's National Gallery of Victoria also holds powerful pieces of North Queensland tribal art.

Rock art was painted on natural walls, with a sheltering overhanging 'roof', in the rainforest not far from Redlynch. The overhang has not provided enough protection of its fragile surface because it is exposed to Wet season rains. Designs were placed on the ceiling for safety. Four female figures were depicted as if running along the wall, as distinct from the static drawings on the Atherton Tablelands (Edwards, 1968, p. 7).

A large cave site was discovered by R. Dalrymple in the ranges between the Murray and Herbert Rivers near Cardwell. Before he was appointed Government Agent General in London in 1872, the geologist Richard Daintree organised for an important photograph to be taken of this rock art site (Bolton, 1969). It may have been the same ceremonial cave visited and recorded by the Governor of Queensland, the Marquis of Normanby, in October 1872. He found it while he was looking for a route across the Seaview Ranges for the telegraph line to the Gulf of Carpentaria. The Governor believed its painted surface to be made from human blood. The cave was not rediscovered, keeping its spiritual significance intact (Brayshaw, 1975, p. 12).

The art of Indigenous tribes is indispensable in the complete history of colonisation. Their careful observations of the new foreign animals were disturbed in the chaos of the Gadja's advance, so the painting of the Giant Horse at Laura—horse at its overpowering front and the tail of a bullock or a pig at the back—embodies awe, fear and a curse.

The similar themes in the rock paintings found at different sites across Australia convey a sense of ancient relatedness of the tribes across the continent. These sites are far apart—at Laura, Ngarrabullgan and Chillagoe in North Queensland, at Mutiwindji in New South Wales and at Olary Province in South Australia.

Engravings also are to be found in south-eastern Cape York; they are pregnant with meaning. Understanding the meaning of the ceremonial Cape York cavern cupule engravings, north of Laura, also suggests the sacred fertility context of cupules at Jinmium in north Western Australia. I think they share the concept and the antiquity of the spotted dolerite rock used in Britain's Stonehenge.

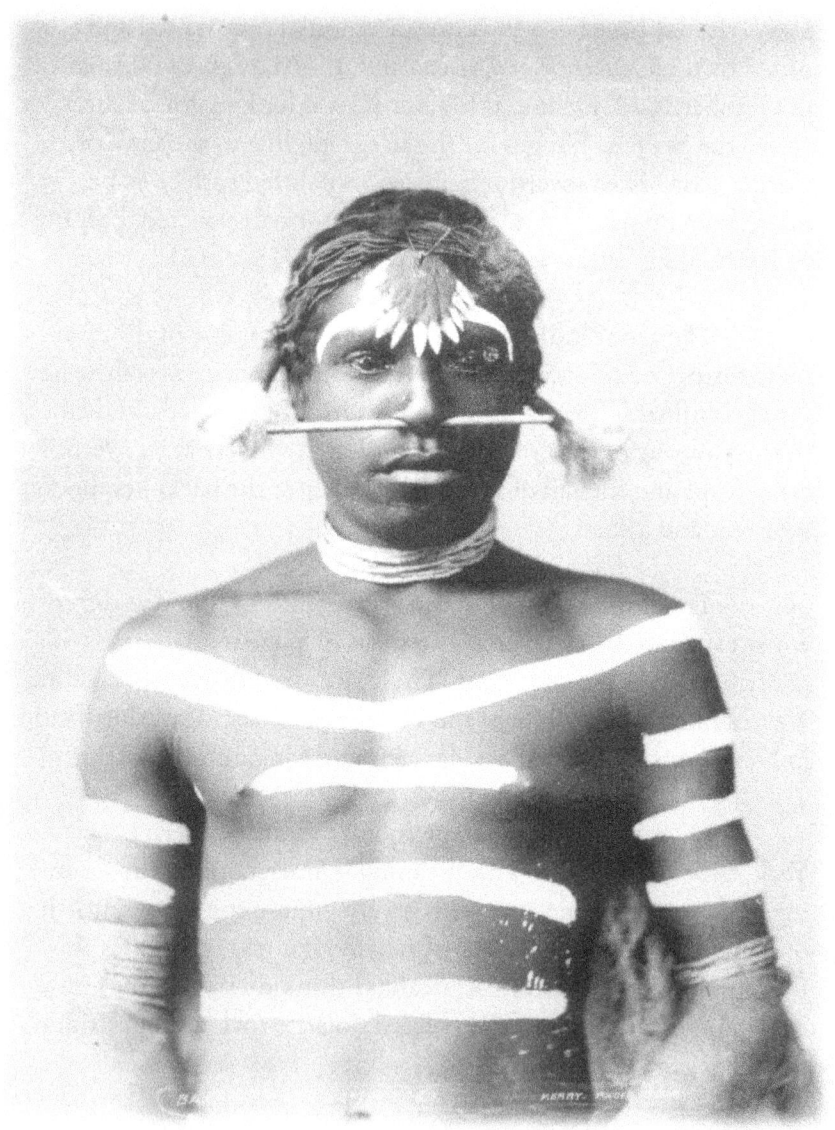

Photograph of Barron River tribesman. State Library of Victoria. Reproduction rights reserved.

The Aboriginal custodians do not want to trade their Storywaters as a commodity, but they do use the public face of the stories (Outside Storywaters) for business, tourists and land rights. Entertaining tourists by performing Aboriginality is real work for the Aboriginal people. Without copyright protection, the Bama may be exploited by the Aboriginal heritage industry of entertainers, artists, writers, curators, environmentalists, rangers, tour guides, archaeologists and anthropologists.

Gadja photographs and pictures of Aboriginal men and women, like rock art, are part of the politics of representation and are as much a record of White colonialism as about Aboriginal culture.

In the magnificent portrait of the young Barron River tribesman, photographed a hundred years ago, his poise and power remain, like a Gauguin portrait.

This photograph was probably taken by Alphonse Chargois, with negatives on glass. He had a photographic studio in Cairns. In 1942 when the Japanese invasion was expected, his family decided to evacuate south and smashed this priceless archive of historic photographs to prevent it being possessed by the enemy. His grandson, writing this to me in a letter, said that the family returned to Cairns in 1943.

The remarkable photograph, which could have been taken as early as 1890, became part of the Charles Kerry collection and then the King collection. It was auctioned for a high price in Melbourne as part of a set. It was described in a book of photographic images this way:

> 'the dramatic artistry of his headdress, nose ornament, necklace and arm bands were apparently insufficient proof of his barbarity; the photographer's negative has been crudely painted with an opaque medium masking the emulsion in broad bands across the young man's torso and upper arms, with a few blots and speckles here and there.' (Moore & Hall, 1983, p. 66)

In an Aboriginal gallery in the heart of Sydney I saw a display of wondrous barks and artefacts for sale. As I walked among them the dealer was on the 'phone to an artist in central Australia, 'Keep on painting! The more dots there are the more dollars. They like your style. Have I seen what they are doing in Cairns? It's just like Miami!' He was conversing long distance with a culture on the perimeter of his own.

A new awareness is arising in photographers of complicity between them and their spectators as voyeurs of an exotic culture. In a 1994 television film, Papua New Guinean native subjects refused to be indiscriminately filmed as simple primitives where a foreign narrator told viewers what the natives were thinking. 'An admiration for their spectacle appears to assuage guilt for destroying their culture' said Les McClaren, the film's maker. With new social concepts working for Aboriginal people, pictures of symbolic violence such as men or women in chains can now be seen as a voyeuristic spectacle of teaching by violence and terror, inherited from the convict tradition.

Intellectual Property

The Bama use song, story and art for their Bulurru, their religion and law, and also for their Storywaters. They relate to a community ownership of its art forms as much as the Gadja do to theirs. Wood, stone or a person's skin was a publishing medium, with no need of paper, when there were over four thousand Bama in the region just north and west of modern Cairns. Descendants remain today and there are just a few elders left with their own copyright. Storywaters are Bama intellectual property; not paper knowledge, but for their hearts.

Initiated people may use their private knowledge of Inside and Outside Stories (what should and should not be said in public) conveyed in their own words. The private knowledge is in its owner's care, and recording rights of ownership must be decided, for cultural links can get lost in performance in the White world.

Aboriginal people 'possess' sung and spoken cultural acts in Bama customary law; this disadvantages them in the written tradition of Whites. Copyright restrictions expire in fifty years or more. Ideas are free but when expressed in words, song or pictures, they can be owned, especially when written down or painted. Protocols apply; see Section 35(2) of the Copyright Act in Australia. To say 'folklore' will not do. Indigenous artwork should be certified, signed, by the artist.

Aboriginal people painted in their cave as their sign of ownership of it. Rock art used to be seen by Whites as being 'in the public domain'. It is easily damaged. Aborigines have difficulty proving their claims as the original artists. Now there are Indigenous moral legal rights over it and also over their genetic material.

A protocol of acknowledgement is the initial and primary etiquette for Aboriginal courtesy and law in interracial relations. They want to prevent the stealing or misuse of their art and culture. For instance, David Malangi's Aboriginal artwork on the one dollar note of 1966 was not acknowledged till much later.

> 'More Indigenous control and utilisation of records in archives is needed to replace the brokerage in transactions between blacks and whites which now occurs. An informed Aboriginal population will have a much greater feeling of power over its own destiny' said Bama academic Dr Henrietta Fourmile.

Indigenous writers and artists are struggling for recognition on whitefella terms. To submit to assimilation into the dominant culture could result in a 'hyphenated' identity of self, alienated from their tribe. The Bama people's defensive feelings about publishing are due to an unequal power relationship where Whites have exploited their collaboration with Aboriginal artists to their own benefit. For example, David Ngunaitponi (Unaipon) of the Ngarrindjeri in South Australia penned his epic on Aboriginal myths and legends from an educated but relatively powerless position. His work was poorly paid, plagiarised and copied. Melbourne University Publishing has now published the original version under the title *Legendary Tales of the Australian Aborigines* (Unaipon, 2001).

'The issue is about plundering our intellectual property and its non-acknowledgment. It is all about integrity and respect,' said Intellectual Property media and cultural heritage solicitor Terri Janke (2005). She published her novel *Butterfly Song* to make her point. Terri went to school in Cairns and completed her law degree in Canberra. She also wants to protect Indigenous art and artefacts from being copied interstate and overseas as souvenirs.

Now with access to the Internet, Aboriginal artists in the country can keep up-to-date with reproductions and with city trends and prices for their work, by following art gallery advertisements and auction results. Similarly, writers can remain informed of their market and check for translations of their work into other languages. Musician writers are also entitled to provenance and to receive payment royalties.

The Copyright Council's website is *www.copyright.org.au*.

CHAPTER 12
FINDING A VOICE

In August 1970, linguist Peter Sutton collected recordings of over seventy five Aboriginal languages in Far North Queensland that were almost extinct, dying at the rate of about one a month. Many Aboriginal people denied knowing a language that they obviously spoke so well. Believing he was a policeman or welfare officer, they hid in toilets or private spaces until he had gone away. He told me they would not speak with him at Darrella. They were afraid of punishment.

By 1976, most Indigenous speakers had died. Sutton had grasped the vital social meaning of language differences for Aboriginal sacred geography and land tenure, but cultural research was not yet familiar in the North (Sutton, 1992, pp. 453–457). Today more people are aware of the struggle to keep Indigenous cultural practices alive.

Sutton said recently that in settlements many young are less emotionally mobile, not confident with strangers. It was a problem to support them while improving their living conditions, including work, school attendance and waste management. Some Murris want to lead modern urban lives (Sutton, 2009).

Their spoken words express the fragile aspirations of Indigenous people. Printed words can be a way of enforcing the cultural invisibility of the 'stolen generation'. Their stories are not known because their voices are muted, but not silent, in texts. They have had to fit their needs for self-expression to new Gadja words and its value system, to new ways of learning.

Roy (on the left) and Don Banning at home in Harvey Road Redlynch, 1993

Bama storyteller Roy Banning told me about the significance of tribal recollections of land and the traditions of Murris settling their differences.

> 'Djabugay history is important to us all in the Redlynch district. We are losing our old people and we want to teach the young people our traditions as much as we can. As part of cultural education through the schools and the community, we can record our talks, say it steady and people can hear the sound; we can keep it and distribute it, one per family, our language first followed by English.

A written record would also help us present a true picture of our life and heritage. We would like to increase the understanding of multicultural relations as new developments are taking place, on land such as Darrella, off Kamerunga Road and Crystal Cascades where we used to live the old life, where our old people were buried. We are looking to the best way for the future of our children.'

Traditionally Murris learnt their culture beside their families as they hunted and gathered provisions, became independent and made relationships. They prefer open doors and windows. In contrast, for Whitefellas,

'To learn in buildings, what you are supposed to do and how, the hierarchy of the teacher out the front of a class is "education" in concrete terms. The frames of a dominant ideology, of thinking, have been translated into tin or brick walls' (Hebdidge, 1979, pp. 12–13).

Murris in Sydney feel at home in Redfern, among Aboriginal people from other regions. 'Most of our "tent embassy" generation are dead now' mourned activist Dr Gary Foley,

'It was rough when I was a teenager many years ago in Redfern. It was a war of attrition with the police. Where could we get books about us? Books about the U. S. civil rights movement taught us to read.'

He was speaking at the forum to celebrate the 1967 referendum for Indigenous people. Now a lecturer in Indigenous Studies at the Victoria University of Technology, Dr Foley says Aboriginal people are trying to take control of their own affairs. Activists should be focusing on the important unresolved political issues like land rights, economic independence and self-determination. The Government's Stolen Generation apology was just part of the need to address White Australia's long history of denial of past discrimination and cruelty and myth of caring for Aboriginal people. The Federal intervention was a policy of assimilation.

When Dr Foley started gathering evidence about abusive treatment, Aboriginal friends said he was just a masochist looking for a good kicking. But information put more bone into his back, power into his thinking and law into his hands.

Finding a voice for shy men and women in an intimidating courtroom is a struggle. When Aboriginal witnesses are interrogated by lawyers in court they may only have a small idea of what is going on, of their legal position, of the importance of the evidence they are asked to give. They may be polite, they want to avoid conflict, agree and get off the stand. It is called gratuitous concurrence, but their evidence is manipulated (Hooper, 2008, p. 98).

Dr Diana Eades (1992) has written *Aboriginal English and the Law: Communicating with Aboriginal English Speaking Clients: A Handbook for Legal Practitioners* and *Aboriginal English in the Courts: A Handbook*. More of her publications for Aboriginal people attending court are listed at www.une.edu.au/staff-profiles/bcss/deades.

The murder of Aboriginal people by white settlers in the 1800s was not the only persecution. It has continued into the twenty first century. There is now the threat of cyber bullying, stalking and defamation on the Internet with malicious harassment on websites. Threats to be killed at home and school, or being bullied with abusive names like 'Abo' and 'Coon', have replaced the shootings in tribal homelands.

Finding a voice

Recently a few Aboriginal students, too frightened to return to school, have pursued compensation claims under new racial vilification laws. The aunt of a young Aboriginal man who was bashed to death has a son intimidated by racial taunts. She said, 'What do I tell him? He's been hurt too much and I don't feel it is our role to go back and educate the school' (*Valley Weekly*, 2005).

In dealing with bullying, Dr Errol West, of the Southern Cross University Education Unit at Lismore, NSW, explained the situation.

> 'We have our heroes. Sometimes we struggle to find those who deal with these issues. I spend hours each day shovelling shit out of Aboriginal kids' faces. We grasped the 1967 referendum vote and used it. If we hadn't, nothing would have happened. Education must engage parents in decisions. It needs objectivity on Aboriginal programs, like Abstudy. Our struggle is not about kids learning, but about politics. Equity is unequal distribution of resources for equal outcomes. Do threatened children and parents recoil? Is this the issue—is it safe for Aboriginal children at school and university with their level of (emotional) baggage and stress of corrugated thinking; are they being forced into further danger? The academy should be about shared power. It turns pessimism to optimism.' (West, 1997)

Richard Trudgen, a resource officer for the Yolngu people of Arnhem Land, has written that 'Naming and blaming permeates dominant culture thinking'. He explains that when people, whatever their colour, feel threatened they do not respond reasonably; they may begin to name, blame and lecture. This behaviour immediately 'blocks the thinking of those involved, and stops any creativity by simply laying the cause of the problem at the feet of the Yolngu' (Trudgen, 2000, p. 62).

An idea that the person is guilty or inferior paralyses the perceptions of that person who is told to change. Victim naming is a form of cultural imperialism that makes the problem worse (Trudgen, 2000, p. 64).

Lockhart River mission women making a mat from dried pandanus leaf for the east wall of the church sanctuary. The cross is made of the same leaf with native dyes.

However, gaining ownership of traditional lands through native title claims, especially on Cape York Peninsula at Lockhart River, has lifted Indigenous spirits. The Queensland Government transferred 354,000 hectares of former crown land to the community in 2001 (Fitzgerald et al., 2008, p. 198).

The greater sense of pride in their Indigenous culture by Aboriginal people and Torres Strait Islanders is reflected in the census figures. In 1996, 2.9 per cent of Queenslanders were self-described this way; an increase of thirty-six per cent since 1991, or almost 25,400 in the Queensland Indigenous population.

With the change in official attitudes to Aboriginal culture, there are now Indigenous Knowledge Centres (IKCs) of Bama family records and histories in the north including the Torres Strait Islands. Written works, oral histories and art are in regional libraries and at the State Library of Queensland in Brisbane. Indigenous librarians help people seeking family history records and government documents (Fitzgerald et al., 2009, p255).

So take heart. Just as there are glass cutters for glass ceilings there are smoke alarms for smoke screens and telephones that are colour-blind to social or ethnic status. A man's prestige is not measured by his height when he stands on his wallet and neither is a woman's status by her bust size.

CHAPTER 13
CIVILISATION AND VIOLENCE

Globalisation brings us into transactions with strangers. We deal with other races. Racism is about differing values; how will strangers treat children, lovers and foreigners? This difference worries like a stone in the shoe, like change (Clark, 1997).

The idea of clothing starts from the feeling of bare feet. After there were trousers, nakedness was political. Wearing clothes is deliberate, for to civilise is to control sensory pleasure and violence, the presence of one inhibiting the other.

Both Blacks and Whites have very different histories to contribute to the Australian identity. On the new Australian frontier, colonial folk bore a European anxiety about lust beneath their sense of daring, arrogance and larrikin confidence. Their relationship with Murris was fraught with passionate feelings about those velvety girls who were often more alluring than mateship, for an undeclared peace movement was taking shape. The hands-on social engineering was deconstructing colour. For their part, the white women felt vulnerable, not so much overjoyed as outnumbered, with wariness about abandonment to pleasure. There were many more men than women and living conditions were often difficult.

Acts of passion and violence in our colonial past can be a disturbing spectacle, but if we are suitably horrified we are no longer responsible. We can look carefully away from contemporary violence and racism. Meanwhile, detribalised 'mixed blood' people, fringe dwellers on reserves, may make an important statement. They take a political decision to stand against incorporation and decay, if they can, in a defence against cultural violence (Cowlishaw, 1992).

> 'Exposure of fiendish powers in the media has normalised ordinary violence. People were more likely to be killed or assaulted two hundred years ago than today. Home crimes are not talked about but nasty true claims are more serious, offered for our outrage if we want to do something about it. Violence is part of the nation's culture, acceptable in men; it may be disclosed by maps of violence where there is a big percentage of Aborigines living in urban ghettos' (Howe, 1996).

We keep ourselves nice by disallowing incest, murder and cannibalism but, God forbid, we each see in the other aspects of ourselves that we do not know at all. Allegations of cannibalism in Australian politics are first about otherness. We can call them names to demonise these disturbing characteristics. 'Savage' is an epithet about the values of an unknown culture. No hard evidence of stone or bone remains has been found to prove the existence of this form of human consumption in Australia.

Stories have remained—like 'Palmer River chop suey'. Eric Mjoberg described bloody encounters between Aboriginal people and Whites and Chinese at the time of the Palmer River gold rush (See Appendix 4). When Carl Lumholtz wrote *Among Cannibals* in the North Queensland rainforest over a century ago, he was not devoured. In fact, those people thought he was crazy and to kill him was to risk the wrath of the spirits (Bottoms, 1990, p. 276). Dr Walter Roth, the Chief Protector of Aborigines (1904–06) said European reports about the practice by the Bama could be exaggerated or confused with the mortuary custom of carrying the loved one's remains about as a grieving ritual. Starvation may have forced them to alter their customs (Horsfall, 1987, p. 71).

CHAPTER 14
WHAT'S IN A NAME?

The living conditions of some Aboriginal people and the associated behaviours was a national shame, said Prime Minister Kevin Rudd in 2009. The year before, his National Apology recognised some wrongs done to Aboriginal peoples in the past.

Shame—of a bad label, slander, cyberbullying and media campaigns—is a like powerful spell; it can keep us away from help, out of school, or out of friendships.

People, families and governments like to keep their good name. They will defend it fiercely, and are ready to shame or label others—'invader', 'Nigger', 'Coon'. In the words of Sir Walter Scott, 'Give a dog an ill name and hang him; and if you give a man, or a race of men (Scots) an ill name, they are very likely to do something that deserves hanging' (Goode, 1978, p. 278).

The police on Palm Island, in a violent, dysfunctional community, were despised by the populace who were confined. Would they not feel the need to be despicable sometimes in their powerless disgust, in their longing to escape, and in the atmosphere of hate (Hooper, 2008, p. 81)? Among the palm trees and the fences on Palm Island, the black community opposed the white community on purpose.

> 'You think we're all abject—well, here's what abject is. Here is chaos and self-destruction, unreason and cruelty. Here are all the things you accuse us of, all those things you're frightened of' (Hooper, 2008, p. 162).

It was in this climate that Mulrunji Doomadgee hanged himself in a police cell in November 2004. He was caught in the conflict and paid the price with his life.

Naming may be called 'labelling', which may create a category, named 'deviance'. Deviants act and believe differently. Or it's all about the pot calling the kettle black. For example, that undeclared peace movement with velvety girls was not a shame but a physical reality in North Queensland. When Ernest Gribble took over running Yarrabah Mission, he was faced with a not uncommon crisis—his brother Bert had strong feelings for another teenager, Jinnah Katchewan, and they had a daughter Susie. Jinnah was the first Gungganydji woman to come to Yarrabah. To maintain the family honour Bert was packed off to New Zealand. Three of Susie's descendants told their secret at the Yarrabah centenary celebrations in 1992, and the family gathered for a reconciliation extension of itself (Scott, 2002a, p. 14).

Murri dancers take great pride in getting their traditional tribal dancing correct, otherwise they might bring shame to their teachers. Tjapukai Park dancers have made their name by being seen with heads of government and royalty. They recognise that prestige is a currency across frontiers as well as other forms of prestige such as land and liquor, money and power. People today feel a bigger gap between the control they have over events and the control they want because they are part of the nation. They do not defer upwards as much with the spread of citizenship (Goode, 1978, p. 125).

Prestige implies control and dignity of outcomes. For example, a Murri spouse's clan standing and totem will affect their prestige and perhaps their economic ranking. Their presenting of authentic knowledge, and male and female speaking and listening positions, depends on their social status. Groups' members can control each other towards a group goal with inclusive names. Values are passed along as adults marry out of clan and culture. Passing on values occurs in both town and country, and when people interact between languages and in the parental, adult and child roles.

For Torres Strait Islanders, shaming and explicit criticism is a highly complex mix of factors of family position, gender and status or age which is not determined simply. A younger female worker who has a high status position in relation to the person she is working with (for example she is an 'aunty') may use shaming as a strategy (Lynn et al., 1998, p. 38).

Tactful indirect 'Sackie talk' is important 'for indicating respect for the person and avoiding embarrassment and shame' (Lynn et al., 1998, p. 43). For some Torres Strait Island participants joking, smiling and laughing is a particular 'island way' which they may use as a method to avoid shame and distress (Lynn et al., 1998, p. 47). This is cultural difference as strength rather than weakness.

Our prestige and dignity are determined by our needs and privileges. Visitors with money are free to sleep in the tropical parks but they seldom do. Backpackers choose hostels and their night clubs; Murris may choose the parks. Townsville parkies, short of cash, used to like to camp in Hanran Park or under the bridge at Ross Creek, where they could feel the excitement and company of the town. They were moved. Any despair and drunkenness of the Whites are thus privatised, while Murris drunk in public are visible, acting out their personal story of Aboriginality.

The competition among classes or occupational groups for esteem is a slow, pervasive and powerful set of forces that may eventually alter the social structure of a country. This feeling of a subclass that it has lost prestige may explain right-wing political leanings, expressed as nostalgia for the good old days (Goode, 1978, pp. 303–4).

The cultural violence of social exclusion causes problems; having more resources gives us a greater opportunity to see others' errors, for they are more visible, when not working or living behind closed doors. Superiors try to organise matters so that they can choose when to be 'on stage' (Goode 1978, pp. 304–5).

Now in the cities problems that used to be dealt with informally, perhaps with force, are often dealt with in committees, where class (prestige) and status (wealth) come in. An association will need a constitution and incorporation to get government funding and handle taxation. Proposing formal changes to the system will meet resistance and scorn from those who want the old rules, especially if they want to know they have the right to their privileges (Goode, 1978, p. 304).

Murris don't want to be kept out of decisions by the costs and by regulations. Mudrooroo (1996, pp. 101, 197), Aboriginal Indigenous Studies lecturer, explained,

> 'The denial of cultural and spiritual heritage and lack of recognition of relationship to the land are the root cause of loss of identity, loss of health, and subsequent degradation....The Aboriginal Legal Services are governed by elected boards, each as an incorporated body to satisfy the conditions for government funding. The staff required cost precious

funds and work under strict guidelines. The travel to annual meetings is also expensive.

To be exclusive you must exclude disadvantaged groups to prevent them from obtaining as much prestige for their qualities or performances, as they otherwise might receive (Goode, 1978, p. 283). Exclusion can be through private or public campaigns, legislation, vilification, formal restrictions, quota, false documents, violence, threats, blackmail or bribery. We may actually be seeing the savage nature of the hidden desire for power.

In a shameful episode in February 2005, officers of the Sea and Air Border Security Service in the Torres Strait failed to equip and to rescue Indigenous patrol workers. This neglect with racist indifference resulted in five people being drowned off Badu Island when their boat, the *Malu Sara*, sank in heavy seas with a false certificate of seaworthiness and no functional navigation system on board. A Government attitude of 'sink or swim' prevailed. It was 'A Totally Avoidable Tragedy', the name of the ABC television programme on 29 June 2009 that exposed this incident. The Saub family successfully sued for compensation and the Immigration Department was fined.

This incident provides ample proof that the racism between white and black in Australia is still active in the country and speaks against the confidence of some Australians that our society accepts Aboriginal people as essential members of the community.

Ambivalence is a skilfully hidden obstacle to learning.

Talent and skill are respected but it is possible to stop talent being trained into skill. The black or white lower-class boy who understands motors might be praised for his skill at repairing them but not be encouraged to think about being an engineer (Goode, 1978, p. 137). While not wanting to invest heavily to get better achievements of the lower classes for them to move upwards, people in advantaged positions have wanted to improve the virtue of those classes, mostly with respect to drinking and sex. They think the poor who failed to strive and achieve confirmed their own higher position and removed their feeling of guilt about exploitation. People higher in the social strata are not willing to pay any more than they do in prestige to get a much higher level of performance, for that might then challenge their own domination (Goode, 1978, p. 146).

For example, the Bama combined function and art in their tools. In the rainforest it would take a man four months to cut and shape a large wooden shield out of the buttress of a fig tree with a stone axe, a work of justifiable pride (and no fossil fuels in use). Decorated shields are cultural icon items today; museums have big collections. However, they used to be undervalued. Collectors expected to pay only a few dollars for them, so how could the Indigenous people be fairly paid for their work? Ron Edwards (1996) has illustrated this in *The Australian Yarn*.

Higher levels of knowledge and work skills are a sign of competence. How old and responsible you are seen to be, as classified by government for age or employment awards, can determine your career choices and independence in race, gender and status (Doran, 1988, p. 79). Women, blacks and the working class can remain classified as minors. Without the prospect of a decent job, young people will not try to get training for one. Discouraged, they redress injustice psychologically (Goode, 1978, p. 365).

The clan leaders of the Yolngu of Arnhem Land have also struggled for dignity and for possession in Native Title proceedings in Gadja law. Their failure left them with feelings of great shame and in danger of insulting the Creator Spirit. The feeling of powerlessness and lawlessness caused many of them to lie down and die (Trudgen, 2000, p. 42).

All these sociological issues can be seen in the life struggles of Eddie and Bonita Mabo. Eddie Koiki Mabo was a Bama hero honoured for winning the legal battle against the legal concept of 'Terra Nullius', vacant land, for his Mer (Murray Island) in Torres Strait. This area is described as the gateway to Australia's north. But the legal battle shortened his life. The High Court decision has been named after him as a mark of national esteem.

Eddie's widow Bonita has continued to fight for recognition and rights. Nowadays she works with the descendants of South Sea Islanders who were kidnapped and made to work the sugar cane fields in North Queensland in the nineteenth century. They were called Kanakas. She is descended from Islanders from Tanna in Vanuatu and a Murri grandmother from Palm Island. She remembers the community which made their homes at Halifax, working the rich canelands.

Bonita put Kanaka history second to Eddie's campaign for Mer land rights, but she too constantly confronted discrimination (Mabo, 2002). She helped establish a memorial to the Kanakas, on the Townsville site where they first landed.

CHAPTER 15

THE POWER OF MYTHS

The country is redolent with transient beings for Aboriginal people. These beings cross from the ancestral to the human side of the time barrier in projected transformations of subject and object. Transforming the common life essence, the ancestors can change outwardly at will. With their transcendental bursts of energy they dissolve and re-emerge (Morton, 1987, pp. 100–101). You can almost feel them soaring rapidly upward on the Kangoli, the morning wind that rises from the Gulf of Carpentaria over the plateau of the Cape York Peninsula, as it heats up. The little white clouds tumble like spinning wheels.

The ancestors in the creation legends of the Lardil people of Mornington Island traversed the Milky Way, a river of stars, as Thuwathu, the Rainbow Serpent spirit, and Gidegal, the Moonman. They marked sites and ceremonies around the Gulf of Carpentaria in the centuries before the flooding of the Gulf, maybe 12,000 years ago, when a peninsula was linked to the island.

Tales of tribal laws for family relations, marriages, parenthood, totems, potent love magic, disputes and weather ceremonies, the coming of ships, people naming the landscape and the killing of missionary Rev Hall in about 1917 are eloquently told by the Lardil tribesman, Goobalathaldin, in his autobiography *Moon and Rainbow* (Roughsey, 1971).

Many Aboriginal storytellers also have celestial stories. They know the Lightning Man strikes the axe on the stone; quick as a flash he draws up the lightning rod to thrust into the clouds and the thunder roars with electrifying charge. There they see coloured plasma flares leap out like serpent tongues above the clouds, a brilliant electrical display of lightning. In fact, pilots of aircraft have sometimes seen these plasma flares but they do not speak about them often.

Budaaji the carpet snake was the sacred Bama image of creative energy from which all life flowed. Just a legend? The finding of the fossil remains of the giant *Wonambi barrieri* snake with a length of up to five metres, dating back to the time when the first people arrived on the continent, gives substance to the Rainbow Serpent Storywater (Scanlon & Lee, 2000, p. 16). Wonambi survived on our 'Sahul land' after it had died out on the other continents.

Our societies regulate themselves with ceremonies, customs, myths and symbols rather than using direct force. Murris and Torres Strait Islanders are empowered by their myth narratives, by renaming their experiences and strengths and ways of healing, including naming injustice and remembering loss (Lynn et al., 1998, p. 7). They cannot bring back forgotten rituals and myths but they can save what they have. They can speak about what is, teach the singing and dancing, and the Storywaters, that were beyond the Gadja field of reference with its alien rituals and artefacts.

The first carers of this land earned the right to tell their stories about it, as well as sharing its use between three or four neighbouring tribes. In the hills, plains and swamps they embedded culture in significant sites such as old trees or rocks which became meaningful beings while the Bama caught possum, kangaroo and turtle. 'How much we know of the secrecy, complexity and sacredness of the stories depends on our ranking in the hierarchy of the tribe' (Bottoms, 1990, pp. 227–228).

The power of myths

A Murri elder explained that when his people listened to the land about them, the ancestors' voices grew stronger. The ancestors handled what was once too hard for the people who respected the moral order in the story. Myths have to change from the reality of the violence and the mysteries of the past to allow the unmanageable out. Stories sleep, waiting, and it is our responsibility to keep them alive. When people cannot live through what life is asking of them, they can go back to the ancestors to help them find a way.

With the awareness that one's life is grounded in eternal stories and motifs, one's own personal story begins to feel enchanted. This feeling gives rise to a love of one's own life that is the cure for narcissism, insecurity and self-doubt. In such re-enchantment we find the dawn of a holistic national imagination (Moore, 1996, p. 238).

An archetypal memory like wind under our wings, lifting, drives a universal longing for such myths. The Bama chose their own scrub hen Jaruka for their tribal survival myth in which she and her consort fly to Djarrugan, their mountain nesting. It looks amazingly like a scrub hen mound and an extinct volcano. It is also called 'the Pyramid' where it rises at Gordonvale.

The power in Bama narratives is in their deciding what to do, to endure through experience. Aboriginal people can gain strength from the Storywaters of the two tribes who came to the Cairns estuary. Two sisters together and two brothers together, were involved in an adventure of heroic survival in crocodile-infested rivers. They could even have been exiled for breaking tribal law.

The founding myth of Jaruka is a drama where the ancestors in the stars shone ecstatically for the heroine in her passionate heartbreak and joy, for she was a girl expecting a child looking for a place to stay. With her sister Bindah, the 'shoulder' she leant on, she lived across the inlet of Trinity Bay at Numbungi. It is the beach where the rainforest on Grant Hill runs down to the rock platforms with its reefs, and there is shellfish to gather (Bottoms, 1990, p. 227).

Jaruka said, 'We must find a "munga", a husband to be a father for my little boy.' They walked along the beach at the hill going to Buddabadoo (Yarrabah). At Gungungi they came upon a rock shelter and spent the night there. Bindah wanted to find food the next morning, but Jaruka said, 'I'm going to make this a painted site with my blood to make it permanent.'

Jaruka was a powerful woman. She mixed blood with ochre; she painted a shield and a spear on the roof of the rock where they had slept. As she prophesied, the design can still be seen today. There she gave birth to Numbai. She smoked him and wiped him with special leaves to bring him good fortune through the spirits.

Then the two women came upon two men so they hid in the bushes with the baby. But in their hurry they left footprints which the men followed and the men said, 'Don't be afraid. We just want someone to speak with us. We haven't seen a woman for ages. We've been fishing on the reef.'

This softened Jaruka's heart. Two birds in the hand were worth four in the Australian bush. She knew that the ancestors were keeping an eye on things, that painting and dancing pleased and entertained them above. The women were approved; they had obeyed their tribal Law against incest and, yes, they took the men as husbands.

Numbai grew up to hunt turtles, dugong, wallaby and cassowary, to like ground nuts and water lilies, to watch the women gather kai kai (food). He grew strong, looking after himself.

'Now I will go to my own country to hunt with the people of Karpa Creek,' he said. He went and became their leader. But first he went back to Buddabadoo to say a farewell to his mother and the others.

His aunt Bindah looked at her camp and sighed; she did not like to be parted from this brave boy, her nephew. 'Stay here; I will gather shellfish, catch lizard, get nuts and many fruits. I will make your favourites.'

Numbai smiled; he knew Jaruka and Bindah very well. Putting his arm around his aunt he looked at her and her husband. 'You are my "Mucha" now. It is my turn to look after you. I make this oath.' And from that day on, when the children were little their aunties and uncles made the decisions for them, having more power than their mothers (Bottoms, 1990, p. 228).

Jaruka was not pleased to lose her son. She stayed behind with her husband. She stamped her foot and said, 'I'm never coming back to this place now.'

Jaruka's mate wanted them to return to Russell River. As they debated they began to grow feathers, for feathers are the emblems of vanishing freedoms, of the power of birds to join the sky and the sun. They became scrub turkeys. Jaruka the scrub hen spread her wings and, followed by her husband, Goyalla, flew over to the extinct volcano which the Gadja call Walsh's Pyramid at Gordonvale. 'Here we can make a mighty big nest'. And they did. It was the Murrgu, the earth incubator nest for their eggs and its name is Bunda Djarruga (Bottoms, 1990, p. 228).

The Bama world view, their relationships between women, men and love magic, their spiritual beliefs, is encoded in the Djabugay myths. Goyalla's brother-in-law, Dummery, is the archetypal younger son, the naughty trickster, who makes one learn from disasters. His idea of himself is determined in opposition to Goyalla, who married Jaruka (Bunda Dummery).

Freshwater Creek has been a favourite swimming hole which Dummery called Gidiri. He told the birds who lived there, in its sweet, cool eddies, that they should find homes, and also campfires and they could also fly away. The cassowary, a large flightless bird, which was called father, Bundarra, was left standing there. Dummery saw he had no wings, so he gave him Gidiri, the creek, as his home. He blew down the fruit, nuts and seeds for him to eat.

In the foundation myth of the neighbouring Yidinji, Goyalla is the good brother who came on a raft (not a canoe) from the north with Dummery. The brothers took two women from the Mulgrave River area. Goyalla would not give either of them to his brother. He made it hard for Dummery who (of course) then made things hard. Dummery made the ricket nuts bitter so that they needed lengthy preparation (Dixon, 1991, p. 10).

Dummery, as Goyalla's brother, was rather lost without him; he went along to a new country and built a nest of palm leaves near Redlynch. He was always up to mischief without Jaruka or Goyalla to restrain him. He taunted a crocodile near the mouth of the Barron River; it bit off one of his legs. He died close to the bed of the river where he lies as a patch of low grass in the shape of a one-legged man (Bunda Dummery).

The Djabugay have incorporated many Yidiny words, and now, Gadja words. The Djabugay language group shares fifty-three per cent of a common vocabulary with the Yidinji and a common stock of dreamtime myths.

Elizabeth Patz (1991, p. 246) lists five Djabugay dialects: Yirrgay, Guluy, Nyagali, Bulway and Djabugay. Timothy Bottoms (1992) maps six nations of Djabugay speakers: Yirrganydji, Guluy, Nyagali, Buluwanydji, Djabuganydji and Gungganydji; I show these on Map 2.

CHAPTER 16
THE BAMA WAY OF LIFE

Bama children were taught early to find their food to survive. Being responsible for the consequences of one's actions was taught by tribal instruction, by example, rewards and punishments. Ceremonies were held to mark the passage into maturity, be it puberty or a seasonal gathering. After initiation, individuals carried a more confident attitude into dealing with later difficulties.

Initiations such as scarring (cicatrice investiture) are stages of bestowing and achieving status and power to handle pain, responsibility, elation, grief, joy, envy and fear. They also acknowledge your ability to obey the Law and care for yourself, your tribe and your country. The higher levels of knowledge about cultural secrets lend sacredness to the spiritual power, against which one cannot fight. Sacred objects prove ownership of the place, the country. Its symbols are chunks of compressed knowledge and power about the cosmos and how people fit into it. To stand up in this place is to find yourself (Anderson, 2001).

Surviving initiation and growing up can be very painful for boys and girls, messy but necessary for psychological development to take place. The adolescent is not immunised against heartbreak, drugs, drink, plastic money and transience without portals of ritual into adulthood. Murri ceremonial scars are badges of honour, indicating bravery over pain and fear, in hunting, or fights or for childbirth. This enables them to look out with assurance on the world and become close to others.

These initiations protect a culture from falling into disarray. Otherwise the culture must find other tests to take their place, such as in camping out, learning to read tracks, school work, job hunting, fighting, sport, dating, driving, drinking alcohol and taking drugs, that have their own rituals, ceremonies and myths.

These portals can give strength to living, or instead be a rite of passage with a term in gaol. In colonial times White felons or convicts with scars felt stigmatised. The Greek word 'stigma' originally meant a pointed mark on the skin, scar or brand of disgrace, of shame. Holocaust Jews with concentration camp numbers tattooed on their arms have a different tale to tell.

Symbols are an observable outline of invisible attitudes. A uniformed policeman drawn upside down by an Aboriginal artist on a rock face at Laura is a sign that means he has been cursed. Or consider the dilly bag, the supreme symbol of woman; when it is drawn upside down it is firstly a sign of no food supply.

The growing popularity of didgeridoo music is part of our national self-acceptance, adopted from the Yolngu of Arnhem Land, where it is called yidaki. Traditionally, the didgeridoo is made by men from long hollowed-out branches and decorated with great feeling by their loving hands.

Today you may see some youngish men and a young woman pucker their lips, loosening them up on the mouths of their didgeridoos. They are tourists from round the world learning to play these long decorated pipes in one of the open shops on the boulevards of tourist spots such as Cairns. They want to play this music when they get home. The forest of woodwinds, all standing up asking to be held, may not be what the European founding fathers foresaw when the settlers first invaded Australia's north. This orchestra of flatulent sounds that the students are learning make the spirits chortle among themselves, for these instruments are supposed to be laid down and only played by men, to keep didgeridoos quiet and to retain their awe.

As with a cello, the melody of a didgeridoo can be sorrowful, and important for carrying pain. Didgeridoos are great symbols of masculinity, a good insurance policy against anxiety and impotence, with their length, deep resonant voice and phallic charm.

To experience Bama culture is to enter the realm of rainforest romance. Their love affairs have their rules in their social calendar. Traditionally the tribe had avoided incest by 'marrying out', moving through different clans at certain times of the year. A man would go and pick a wife from a different area and she would mostly go back to where her husband was from. The children were brought up there with their moieties and animal totems and it kept going that way. Donald Thompson (1972) describes Wik and Koko kin classifications on Cape York Peninsula.

Bama kinship is as structured as that in European royal families. Not long ago women's husbands were chosen for them, but today they have more freedom. However, when a girl goes back to the clan for a marriage partner, she can't be seen formally with any of them; they are all extended family. As my informant explained the details, it sounded like a television soap opera:

> 'A lot of incest is happening today. You don't even know who is who. Cousins' marrying was against the Law. They try to keep it, but they may be ignorant or it can't be helped; a child is there. For instance, a father-in-law is a wife's cousin and his mother is the wife's sister, about three ways of being cousins. That is very wrong by the rules in the old days, but is being accepted now. It would have been punished before.

'This "Skin" or family story is in fact a genealogy. Take a woman with a baby and move her from Mareeba to Mona Mona when the mission is set up, about 1913. She has her full blood or mixed race children there with her but keeps visiting the old Places. She has been given to a Ngarrabullgan husband who dies. She goes to the area again and meets and marries another man from that tribe. Her son has two other "mothers" as well as powerful uncles and aunts, who may all remarry. There are now many birth, marriage and death certificates on which a white registrar has put thumb prints for those who could not write.

'To get out of a place like a mission Aborigines had to have a certificate, what they called "dog tags". It states on the paper that they were "civilised". With the thumbprint, the official wrote "has been conformed". Hard racist words—"father white man, mother Abo"—disturb the Bama and they don't want it to happen to their children.'

Now Deoxyribonucleic Acid (DNA) analysis can tell more than who you are; it can tell who your folks were too. The discovery of DNA blueprints may revolutionise family histories and biological archaeology. The sorcerer's concept of magical use of body parts to curse or charm has evolved from his extra-sensory intelligence into the science of pathology. People can also be identified by marks on the body.

> Our true life tales are never read
> As Murris keep it in the head.
> Bodies tell how blood will show
> History's writ on Bama though.

The Bama way of life

It's smoko. A young Djabugay woman offers me tea while her daughter plays on the verandah. She is telling me about Quinkans; Quinkans are thin invisible spirits that hide in the dark and rock crevices, and have sorcery powers for good and ill. They can be tall or short.

This mother feels always that someone is there on an old house site she goes to, even though there is no house there at all now. The tribe pulled it down to chase away the Quinkans, yet her uncle and his dog felt they were attacked there by something. With a piece of softwood, like driftwood, one is armed to scare away these bad men or evil spirits. I began to want one too for a spooky presence as she continued to tell her story.

'Softwood is like driftwood and it breaks apart in your hand, but you hit the evil one on the head with it and they run away. They're awful, very smelly. They smell like they're dead, rotten. My aunt used to work up at Laura, that's Quinkan country, and believes they walk along the rivers and the roads; some of her family are still up there. People feel quarrels, that they are attacked when they have been drinking.

'Something keeps coming out where our old aunties used to stay. Elders call them "Guingans"; maybe strangers hang about. Quinkans are still believed to walk over there from Cooktown or down to this country looking for a wife and children. Even now people up there have a strong belief; it is even painted into their art.

It's the story they tell every day at Split Rock in the part where you come up the steps—a Quinkan near a wife and husband upside down; that is sorcery for "they're dead". If the paint is brownish, that's normal, if it is yellow they've been caught by witchcraft. You also see a man painted not far from there with six fingers. Even clever Quinkans come down here (south) looking for wives. Those beliefs get handed down through the generations and the hand stencils are still to be seen at Laura.

'There is a track to the rock art at Bare Hill, at Speewah, but Grandfather keeps it secret. The Quinkans think that is best; it protects the paintings and engravings. Down on the coast you find the Hairy Man who is the sorcerer. The "Tamborine" Bama, out Mt Garnet way, Mt Ballibo, have the same belief about the Quinkans'.

When you are a young girl spiritual beliefs can be scary, better kept a secret. Two sisters went fishing in the Archer River there one day with a Mum and Dad in the Nissan; they were about thirteen and ten years old. They said a big Hairy Man like a yeti chased them while they were in the car, a gigantic shadow coming towards them. They just panicked; it was right at the back of this ute that wouldn't go very fast. The Quinkan started running, making funny noises, and they just cried in fear. Of course their Dad thought they were just playing round, for they were always talking about Quinkans. Mum told Dad to hurry up—it was just going on to dark—which is just the perfect time for evil spirits.

Bama young people have their own tales of the bogey man; I was entrusted with this story. This is part of a girl's register of knowledge, uncontaminated by Gadja history.

Didgeridoo phantoms can also haunt a girl if they are shut up in a room with her. They choke her and pull off the blankets. Nor do they want to hear clapsticks played loudly without ceremony. It is very wrong to do that just anytime like it is done today, and when sacred rules are broken they make the devil of a fuss.

CHAPTER 17
WOMEN'S BUSINESS

'Women had more power in a war than men', said Kelvin Hill passionately and the writings of Norwegian anthropologist Carl Lumholtz begin to reveal why. While in Australia, Lumholtz noticed that older women took a very active part in tribal conflicts in the rainforest. Relations between male and female intrigued Lumholtz who wrote a detailed history of a prolonged camping visit to north Queensland. He was principally near Herbert River, about 180 miles to the south of Cairns, where the culture of the Bama also prevailed (Lumholtz, 1888, p. 138). A significant collection of artefacts from the visit is held in Oslo, Norway.

> 'The robbery of women as property is both the grossest and most common theft, the usual way of getting a wife (Lumholtz, 1888, p. 138). Many a woman changes husbands on that (fight) night. As the natives frequently rob each other of their wives, the conflicts arising from this cause are settled by borboby, a fight, the victor retaining the woman ... If one of the men is conquered, the old women gather round him and protect him with their sticks, parrying the sword blows of his opponent, constantly shouting "Do not kill him" (Lumholtz, 1888, p. 135) ... They beat the ground with their digging sticks, urging, crying out four or five to each man, who gets wildly excited. Perspiration pours from them, exerting themselves to the utmost' (Bottoms, 1990, p. 251).

The women could make their own dwelling of palm leaves and hunt and gather their own food before they became dependent on mission stations. In their way of life they used to have more social and economic power than white women had. The Bama's belief that women were in charge of a lot of the love magic, and therefore had informal control, is what women's magazines have been implying for years!

Each Bama group controlled sexuality by thresholds and initiations with their own significance, children's games being seen as part of normal development. Providing was a big part of the male role. Tribes around Cairns were reported to believe that the acceptance of food from a man by a woman was the actual cause of conception. (Countless couples today will swear this is true.) Another local story was that a special kind of pigeon brought the new baby to the mother in the course of a dream (Bottoms, 1990, p. 273). That is rather like the stork delivery myth of Northern Europe. Babies were betrothed at birth to someone selected from an opposite moiety or totem. A girl might often have a shoulder scar as a reminder of affection.

Social strategies basically revolve around male/female relationships, which are in turn linked to competition between lineages for control of labour (Hodder, 1986, pp. 5, 53). Women's control of childbirth is integral to their status, whether planting the seed is virility or planting the placenta is about being joined to the earth. The women of vanquished tribes know they carry their genetic heritage on; it is in the cells in their genes (Thorne, 1995). It is practical reconciliation in bodily form, a passing on of war or peace to their descendants, a means of survival once there were men in trousers.

The female head of household is a continuing influence in a society that is often called a patriarchy, although fathers were separated from their children much more than the mothers were. Self-reliant Bama matriarchs in households with incomes and pensions may have real power. However, having money also means having White tensions between spouses as women claim more control over the cash than men are willing to allow. Some of the women are seeking liberation from a double oppression of White misconceptions and degradation without causing further injury to the Black man, for a man may feel more powerless than an abused woman.

The concept of the 'supporting mother' is an Australian archetype, built into the underlying struggle for control of our national culture. Just as the Bama depended on the women to leach out the toxins from the cycads and other starch foods, they have relied on the women to cook. These women show the way to care for country and kin today. They have the prestige and the responsibility that their Law confers with that custody and its surviving cultural links. Grandmothers Law still has a place, with access to traditional experience and deeper meanings.

The State's permitted activities are powerful signifiers of who can procreate, and who keeps the nation going. Laws 'protect' women but they are really about allocation of property, not about violence in marriage or autonomy. Aboriginal Rights leader Evelyn Scott, a prominent North Queenslander, has campaigned for protection in law from domestic violence and sexual abuse of minors. In defence of her daughters, she refused to put racial loyalty above the law.

However, the social violence in Cape York settlements has demanded change. Young women such as Tanya Major, as a practising criminologist, are leading the way. She comes from Kowanyama, in the north west of the Cape. She maintains that 'it is not right that going to prison has become the male right of passage'.

Indeed, some young women are learning how to tackle different issues. They have done their homework the White way. Armed with theoretical weaponry they are decision-making adults. In 1992 it showed. The Native Titles Act had just been passed. At the end of the International Rock Art Congress in Cairns the Annual General Meeting of over one hundred professional scholars, scientists and artists was convened. After days of every avenue of the art being explored, they were all ready to wind up and catch their planes overseas.

The 'business arising' was solidarity, moved by Dr Henrietta Fourmile:

> 'We want a motion of support for Indigenous people from the assembly please, not by mail order, not by a subcommittee from the halls of learning, not from overseas, now before you go.'

Ahem. Shuffling; an unprecedented international event of commitment. A moment of silence. The more reasonable she seemed the more harassed they appeared.

Yes, now,' said the Murri ladies. They were not coons, boongs, wogs, dagos or poofs. They spoke for the Third World.

The flights were waiting.

'Yes' said the meeting.

When you are really seeing and not just being looked at, and some things are explained to you, you have a lot of power over the world. You can take naming, a way of stabilising knowledge, apart. An over-reaction by Aboriginal people to be not what Europeans are is like feminists substituting reversals of sexist categories of leadership and control even if they don't work. The powerful move is to displace and upset what may count as knowledge where it matters. Getting hold of what is true and real, and sharing their meanings among themselves is women's secret business, which keeps their culture strong (Wolf, 1991).

CHAPTER 18
MEN'S BUSINESS

The Bama men want the legal right to free speech with moral integrity and human dignity as full citizens. They share tribal roles with their women, their dramatic and directional dominance, in their men's and women's business. Fathers are very important and show deep parental affection. Traditionally they did not strike their children for they might then lose courage, but there were wife-beatings and domestic fights.

Dr Mick Dodson, 2009 Australian of the Year, urged indigenous men to own up to their domestic violence before it destroyed them and their families, and to have more respect for their womenfolk and to share parenting responsibilities. Men who felt they have gone from warriors to victims under the impact of colonisation must not remain 'men behaving badly'. Mick Dodson said 'We cannot use historical factors as an excuse for unacceptable behaviour' (Dodson 2002).

To feel your father's arms around you is the greatest gift of patriarchy, its secret purpose in the generations. Fathers like to show their love for children through providing food and shelter, with evening story telling about family rules, and what is expected.

With the absence of fathers due to separation, work or bad health, Murri men have to find their feet as best they can, in town or in country, in or out of work, in their relationships with women and then as parents. What should a father be? Should he be seeking welfare, or native title? What does it mean to be able to drink alcohol even though it has bad effects? To be the supporting partner means abdicating from the traditional prime focus—the brave risk taker.

Traditionally death was the punishment for sexual intimacy between family members. To avoid incest, marriage relationships were carefully controlled. Today however, with people crowded into reserves and settlements and fewer eligible marriage partners, Murris cannot always abide by their own Law of skin, moiety and clan. Shame at breaking one's own Law may lead to destruction of self or property, a story within the apparent new freedom.

Intermarriage with other tribes since the coming of Europeans has complicated boundaries for land use and seasonal migrations and causes disputes between dialect groups. Overlapping tribal zones and the taking of other women affects native title and individual land claims, setting family against family.

Aboriginal men worry that mixed-blood children may be deprived of their paternal inheritance rights to their ancestral country, even though they may have rights through their mothers to both country and ceremony. They may also be denied their inheritance rights from White parents.

When a Murri forms a relationship with an insider they receive the benefit of the insider's status. If a Murri forms a relationship with an outsider the outsider has to be given a status within the Murri's community. The outsider has to find themselves a network of new relatives. It is an old story; their offspring have to earn acceptance, as Steven and Mona did, with multiple parents.

The fight for economic and cultural survival has drawn Murri rural and urban men and women together. Members of the different tribes find themselves living closer to one another than previously. Aboriginal kin identity is not compatible with postcolonial individualism, even in an expanding black underclass. The strength of the campfire group, the skin family of relatives, has persisted in geographic networks, by which the family can avoid isolation from each other.

Murri men always have been responsible for many of the rich ritual and ceremonial traditions as well as for hunting game and for defence. The artistic appreciation of the female figure in Murri art is reflected in the curves of bicornual baskets made by men as a specialty of this coastal region. The design endows sophisticated, powerful enchantment to the women's task of leaching out plant poisons.

CHAPTER 19
THE FIRST PEOPLE

From the huge Sunda Shelf of South East Asia, people came to the Sahul Shelf of Australia and New Guinea some 40,000 years ago where food could be found along with giant serpents and birds of paradise.

They may have dispersed rapidly all over Australia in as little as two thousand years after initial landfall, as the American anthropologist Dr Joseph Birdsell said in 1957. This may yet prove closest to the truth, according to archaeologist Professor Jim Allen (1989, p. 151) who continued Dr Birdsell's research in New Guinea.

Encouraged by rising seas and volcanic eruptions, rafting expeditions followed monsoonal winds and currents far to the east and south. They navigated by the stars and the birds and steered by raising and lowering daggerboards — an Austronesian innovation — between the logs of the raft.

Proof of their Pacific route to America was the discovery by surveyor Percy Fawcett in about 1920 of a wooden deity figure, their souvenir from Easter Island. This silent testimony left behind by our argonauts was disclosed by his son Brian Fawcett (Fawcett, 1953, pp. 244-245).

The skeletal remains of aboriginals have been found at Sierra da Capivara in north eastern Brazil and at Tierra del Fuego in southernmost America. Their pit huts, sometimes built on middens, were like the North Queensland ones, covered by branches.

French archaeologist Anne-Marie Pessis has found some of their skulls and rock art (Pessis, 2000). Among the skulls was the oldest human skull unearthed in the Americas dated by Dr Walter Neves, of the University of Sao Paulo in Brazil, at between 11,000 and 11,500 years ago.

The skull belonged to 'Luzia', a woman in her early twenties according to Dr Joseph Powell, of the University of New Mexico, who has examined hundreds of similar skeletons. According to Neves and Powell, Luzia's skull has distinctive features similar to Australian aborigines and sub-saharan Africans, but unlike the flatter-faced "Mongoloid" people typical of later American migrants (Hayes, 2010).

Neves and Dr Michael Heckenburger have since discovered ancient mudbrick towns, also in the forests of north eastern Brazil (Neves and Heckenburger, 2010).

Professor Silvia Gonzales, a Mexican palaeontologist at Liverpool John Moores University in the UK asks us to consider whether people related to the Australian aborigines were the first to inhabit the New World (Gonzales, 2006/2010). Did they die out, or was this first population overwhelmed by or incorporated into later migrations from Asia?

A ground-breaking survey of the Bama in the North Queensland rainforest was undertaken by Dr Birdsell and South Australian Dr Norman Tindale during 1938 and 1939. They recorded details and took photographs of the Bama people and eventually explained who the Bama were and their heritage. Today these photographs are invaluable for family identification and genealogy (See Appendix 1). By putting names to the Bama faces now, they are again people in control of their self-respect and identity, with re-established boundaries as persons.

As Noel Pearson has said, 'If I tinker with the identity of White Australians, see how far I'd get'.

Dr Birdsell was in awe of the genetic makeup and the physical presence of the Djabugay. He called them 'a small people'. The males were not above sixty inches (or 152 centimetres), with crisp crinkly short dark hair. He had a tri-hybrid theory of them having Murryan/-Barrinean heritage rather than being like the 'Carpentarian' people. Birdsell wrote 'They look like Tasmanian Aborigines'. Their neat physique then is part of their identity, adapted over generations to the rainforest. These twelve small tribes had a pre-contact population of about 3,000, on Birdsell's estimate (Loos, 1982, p. 92).

New research in biological anthropology says the Bama have an older, greater blend of genes, more mixed blood groups. While the Bama may now want to say 'we're not from a zoo to use for your benefit', Birdsell's detailed work supports their identity and long occupation of the rainforest habitat. The work is seen today as racist by Murris, but it makes the Bama's significance in anthropology indisputable. Birdsell and Tindale's photograph collection includes Tommy Palmisland who was able to find that Tambo was his father or his grandfather through this family history. Tambo was one of the Aboriginal men who were taken on a painful tour as cannibal exhibits at circuses in Europe and America around 1884 (South Australian Museum, 1999, p. 4).

Archaeologist Peter McAllister (2010) journeyed to see how the small people of Yarrabah are related to pygmy people around the world.

Dr Birdsell's research included navigating the Torres Strait coastline, which had been visited by explorers from Europe and Asia.

In December 1605, a Spanish expedition with two ships and a tender set sail to discover the land they believed linked up with the end of South America. Portuguese navigator Pedro Fernando de Quiros was chief pilot of the *Capitana*. Meanwhile the other ship, the *Almaranta* was captained by the Spanish navigator Captain Louis Vaes de Torres. Captain Don Diego Prado y Tovar, a Portuguese navigator was also on that ship. Both ships found the islands which are now known as Vanuatu.

When de Quiros found the islands he believed they were the Great South Land they'd set out to discover. He called the islands La Austrialia Espiritu Santo (the Austrian Land of the Holy Spirit) to honour the Spanish King who belonged to the House of Austria.

After spending some weeks in the islands of Vanuatu, the ships separated. Historians give several reasons why de Quiros and his crew returned to Mexico and left Torres and Prado y Tovar in the region of Vanuatu. Some say there was a mutiny on de Quiros' ship and he had to return to Mexico. Others say Torres had sealed orders from the Viceroy of Peru. His ship made its way to Manila in the Philippines, a Spanish colony at the time.

Historians debate whether Torres followed the south coast of New Guinea or saw the north coast of Australia, but the voyage produced surveys and maps of the region. This was most secret intelligence for the Europeans. It was so valuable that Torres's report was hidden in Spanish archives to prevent other European countries from using the information to their advantage. Torres was belatedly recognised as being the first recorded European to sail through the Torres Strait in 1606. However, the information made its way around Europe and the strait between the islands of New Guinea and Australia appeared on maps produced much later by Dutch cartographers.

In 1606 the *Duyfken,* a Dutch ship, visited the west coast of Cape York searching for the South Land. While travelling down the coast, its crew had a fight with the Aboriginal men over interfering with their women.

Asian mariners had been to the Great South Land earlier—to their fabled 'land of parrots'. Chinese ancestors appear to have been with the Bama; a 1421 Chinese global seafaring expedition fleet has been recorded (Menzies, 2002). Emperor Ying Teung produced a porcelain map of the coastline after Admiral Cheng Ho's voyage (Loney, 1993). These Chinese mariners built low pyramids to read the star positions, charting the world. There is one at Gympie.

Below a natural 'pyramid' at Gordonvale there is an exquisite century-old Chinese altarpiece in the Mulgrave Shire Historial Society museum. An Asian god had arrived there. However, the later Chinese in north Queensland built their main temple Hou Wang Maiu near Atherton, completing it in 1903. Seeing the morning mists as the dragon's breath, they blended Taoism and Buddhism with the local spirituality and sited the temple to get the most energy from the landscape and gardens for long life and health. The temple banners ask for reverence and a mind at peace.

Rock engravings of figures like Egyptian deities surmounted by sun discs have been recorded in several parts of Australia, suggesting a visit by their mariners. They would have come for Australian eucalyptus resin, which was used for mummification rites in Egypt. Khunmhotep, an explorer two and half thousand years ago, had told of minerals, mainly copper, and animals which kept their young in their pouches. He was a court official of the Twelfth dynasty with his male partner Niankhkhum. His tomb was found at Saqqara in 1964. An ironstone idol found at Gympie is like the Egyptian god Thoth (Kamrin, 1998).

The best evidence for a visit by Egyptians or Phoenicians is the bronze coin found near Kuranda in dense rainforest by Andrew Henderson, when he was sinking fence post holes in 1911. It was identified by experts in Brisbane to be thirty grams in weight, three and a half centimetres wide, and minted in Barce, Cyrenaica, during the reign of Pharaoh Ptolemy the 4th, who ruled from 221 to 204 BC (Gilroy, 1981, p. 9).

CHAPTER 20
LOOKING AFTER THE COUNTRY

'Look at your clean air and no pollution!' gasped the bank accountant in Izmir, Turkey, when I showed him my photograph of the view from the Kuranda range. Seeing the crocodile corroboree picture, he was momentarily lost for words, but then carefully translating word by word, he grieved for what 30,000 years of occupation had done to his Anatolia. 'Look what we have lost! But how much we would have to give up!' he sighed.

Lloyd Grigg was a crocodile hunter who could see the need to change white men's ways for wildlife conservation. With Vince Vlasoff, Lloyd built the unique underwater coral observatory at Green Island which opened in 1954 to show tourists wonders of the Great Barrier Reef.

Lloyd Grigg with crocodile skin and eggs 1957

A living archaeology

The observatory has shown millions of visitors the importance of marine life for understanding habitat and diversity.

Australians are beginning to try to save our heritage through such actions as the World Heritage listing of the Daintree Rainforest National Park in 1988 and the Barrier Reef Marine Park.

In the 1950s, I explored the reef with film crews from overseas who showed me the world heritage, fascinating and rare species and changes.

Brad Congdon (2009), Reader in Ecology at James Cook University, reported that a survey of the bird population on the significant location of Michaelmas Cay on the Reef found that it had been halved, probably due to the decrease in available seafood for the birds.

Aboriginal people had a cleaner atmosphere in a low carbon economy. Queensland native houses of palm leaves and branches used up little 'embodied energy' with no harmful carbon dioxide given off. Firing a single brick uses as much energy as driving six kilometres in a six-cylinder car, not including its construction and transportation. Drying a load of washing in an electric dryer generates more than three kilograms of greenhouse gases. Alongside coal-fired power and combustion engines, some thirty per cent of Australia's ozone-depleting global-warming greenhouse gas emissions come from land practices such as farming, land clearing and forestry.

Sea levels in the Pacific Ocean have risen millimetres in the last decade. Coral atolls and coastlines could be devastated by the predicted rises, as has happened before. Surface coral only grows at between twenty degrees and thirty degrees Celsius. The rise in carbon dioxide from increased ultra violet light and heat not only bleaches coral but makes the water more acid. This makes it harder for the algae to support the coral animal's skeletal framework which gets weak and begins to die. The food chain of animals is destroyed (Smith, 2001).

In 2001, the Australian Commonwealth Scientific and Research Organization (CSIRO) predicted that by 2070 there would be up to thirty-five days per year over thirty-five degrees Celsius in Queensland, as well as an increase in extreme rainfall by 2030 (Fitzgerald, 2009, p. 277).

A living archaeology

A Category 5 cyclone occurred in March 2006, devastating 17,000 square kilometres of farmland in Innisfail, Atherton and the Atherton Tablelands. An army of workers and volunteers rallied to help the survivors in the disaster. They were all without electric power lines, telephones, computers, appliances like refrigerators, working petrol pumps and money from automatic teller machines. They struggled with roofless houses and food queues during six weeks of torrential rain (Fitzgerald, 2009, p. 260).

In contrast, the Bama are familiar with the condition of being without the use of electric power and facilities that require electricity. More extreme weather conditions may prevail in the future as a result of climate change. *The carbon emissions of the Bama are very low.*

You can imagine the result of a rise in sea levels by considering the effects of cyclones on the landscape. Category 5 cyclone Mahina struck across Princess Charlotte Bay in March 1899 with winds up to 280 kilometres per hour. A storm surge reported to be five metres above the highest tide combined with massive waves to create a tropical deluge that swept kilometres inland.

Hundreds of pearling luggers and boats were lost with their crews. The water and wind killed some 400 people including Aborigines, South Sea Islanders and eight Whites. Two black women swam for ten hours with children on their backs, but the children were dead when they got to safety. (McHugh, 2003, p. 219) The flooding left tons of dead fish, fowl and reptiles on land, and rocks weighing tons were thrown up on land. At Flinders Island, thirteen porpoises were found 4.6 metres up the cliff (McHugh, 2003, p. 221).

Higher temperatures will affect all the animals. In the past, rainforest isolation protected unique species like Lumholtz's tree kangaroo, which was found only between the Herbert River and the Daintree River areas to the south and north of Cairns. Tree kangaroos are marsupials and are the only kangaroo which can move its legs independently to walk. Another unique species is a small shy wallaby that survives at the Paleranda wildlife reserve.

Of all the local birds that are in danger of disappearing today, the magnificent crested cassowary is the biggest. It is a source of food and legend for the Indigenous people. Contrary to most bird species, it is the male cassowary which fulfils the parenting role by looking after his eggs and chicks. Street names are their memorials.

The white-tailed rat and musky rat kangaroo are animals that also used to make the most of stored nuts of the rainforest trees. Even though the nuts contain toxic alkaloids, by the beginning of the Wet season in December, the animals could have stored knee-high mounds of nuts to see them through for several months. The Bama controlled the rat population with their dogs. Sugar cane farming has reduced the rats' survival as they have been found to carry leptospirosis, a liver disease affecting humans.

Flocks of white owls also ate the rats, but these birds have become rare with the baiting and clearing of old trees that contained their nesting hollows. The owls earn their keep when farmers replace tree hollows with nest boxes and stop baiting.

Walking tracks through the rainforest were kept clear by Indigenous control burns which have since stopped. As a result, the rainforest is growing back into the area where eucalypts had begun growing, according to Yidinji environmentalist George Davis (Low, 2002).

However, rainforest narratives still unfold in the evening cool, as they once did when the grey-faced fruit bats (now endangered) would squabble, the curlews cry mournfully and the sparks of the campfire rose with myths towards the stars. When you move about in the night scrub you may leave an iridescent trail of tiny glowing insects, geckos may bark and a few tree frogs croak seductively and try to catch enough moths. A new Kuranda species of tree frogs has been discovered, but their population numbers are shrinking.

In recent years, curlews have multiplied and are seen in parks and gardens in the beach area. They are very quiet birds and unafraid of humans.

CHAPTER 21
A LIVING ARCHAEOLOGY

Tribal discipline and its norms controlled the lives of the many extended Aboriginal families. People would take the time to build kin, a family network of contacts, to belong no matter what. Yirrganydji writer George Skeene (2008) remembers gathering pipis and other shellfish on the beach at Yorkey's Knob with his mother and grandmother. They continued a traditional activity that had been passed on to each new generation. Large quantities of shellfish were gathered mostly by the women. Aboriginal people were still camped on the seafront near the hospital a century ago and the middens were in use till the 1930s.

What materials from this way of life, that still remain, will preserve the Bama social history and its technology? Their artefacts are congealed social labour, and embodied emotional homework. It is 'soft' or 'hard' material culture, such as Grandmothers' Law, their grinding stones, men's four-pronged fish spears or their ground-edge axes.

Murris can understand the point of archaeology and ethnography if these studies help to substantiate their rights based on family recollections. This archaeology and the ethnography alone show how the environment, the Bulmba, controlled their way of life and how the Aboriginal people constructed their world (Peterson, 1993). Archaeology's active involvement in a more scientific and political agenda makes this discipline relevant, addressing issues formerly ignored and avoided (McBryde, 1986, p. 13).

Archaeologist Roger Cribb overlooking an escarpment on a walk near Ngarrabullgan in 1992

With a radio-carbon date of 37,400 years for the base of a rock shelter at Ngarrabullgan, 200 miles north of the Barron Falls, Storywaters get a place-and-time (David, 1993, pp. 50–54).

The decline in conifer-dominated rainforest and a charcoal layer in the pollen core of Lynch's Crater at Bromfield Swamp (near Upper Barron), is radio-carbon dated at 38,000 years ago (Kershaw, 1993).

Then, by 3,000 years ago, green flakes of obsidian, a rare natural glass, were being produced for cutting tools at Echidna's Rest, Nolan's Creek, near Chillagoe (David et al., 1992).

A living archaeology

Bromfield Swamp

Today a pre-historian, or a physicist, can see a whole world in an old grain of sand or stone tool. The new ball game of particle physics dating is presenting us with ever-so-tiny balls. Accelerator mass spectrometry can tell us much more about economic systems, dates, health and social change when we ask the right questions (Allen, 1996) such as when and why it is important. Great social history is embodied even in old grinding and cooking stones and camp fires.

With portable grinding stones, fixed working sites are not needed, but these artefacts become important evidence of social networks and exchange, as their origins can be found. One particular ancient Bama grinding stone belonged to Buttercup Banning's mother. Buttercup herself kept it safe, she told Kelvin Hill, who told me this story:

'The Bama lived on what they called Firefly Mountain, the southern rampart of which was Tigal Peak, below which their ancestor Tegal was born (near Redlynch). The high peak is called Warkmundji (or Mount Williams) and migratory trails run through from Mareeba to the coast. A hundred years ago Buttercup went down the trail for food trees and fruit. She went out of the high country at the start of the Wet to come back after the first storm to the arranged marriage. Girls were picked out when they were very young and had to marry who they were chosen for. She had no choice, she said, with a little laugh. Her chest was ceremonially scarred. She was married tribally at the end of 1911 or early 1912 to Tambo.

'Their son Gilpin Banning, named after the Banning cane farming employers, was born in September 1913, and they also had a baby who was buried at Crystal Cascades. This tribal grave site is where the tribes met on the trails through the jungle and the gorges. After they had Gilpin, they migrated over the Lamb Range for corroborees and fights.

'Gilpin said, "We all met. We knew they were coming weeks before by the smell of the smoke of their fires. We went gathering nuts and turkey eggs, kai kai (food), and ricket nuts (cycads) for grinding."

'Buttercup and her sister Daisybell were two of the few survivors of the Speewah massacre of about 1887. They escaped by asking for a drink of water and to cool a burn from cooking stones. They fled to Crystal Cascades down the mountain when they saw the native police shooting up the camp.

'When Granny Buttercup was a frail old widow wandering, it was Kelvin Hill who brought her home, got her a dress, bathed and fed her. He knew how hard it was for her to walk because she had a hurt back and shoulder from being thrown through a window. On her last trip she got ready to go to number three tunnel. She got away from the camp through the scrub straight up as far as number two tunnel. Kelvin and some of the young people searched. They couldn't find her for a long time but eventually brought her back' (Hill, 1993)

Detail from Laurel Hall. *Buttercup Banning and granddaughter, Redlynch*. Circa 1965. Private collection, Tully. Used by permission.

Mona Fagan then looked after Buttercup at Oak Forest, near Kuranda, for six months. At Redlynch again, Buttercup had to look after herself. After reaching a great age, she ended her days at Yarrabah where she is buried (Fagan, 1996). Buttercup may have suffered from a neurological disease caused by plant poisons eaten in ground-up nuts. See Appendix 3.

British archaeologist Ian Hodder (1986, pp. 5, 53) has said that in archaeology the re-use of dead persons' remains to legitimate access to resources, as a framework of meaning, must be considered. As an example, the Bama used symbolic power in their grieving process for the carrying about and burial of their dead people's bones. It follows from this that the grandparents' burial places at Darrella (at Redlynch) in the foothills have been claimed as sacred sites in a development area on the former campsite.

Murris want greater respect for their ancestors, and reject the desecration of exposed skeleton burial displays. They want bones and mummies returned from museums. In August 1996, an 1860 female mummy and also a skull of a Barron River Aboriginal person were buried in the centre of Cairns at the Anderson Street cemetery with a Christian ceremony. The mummy had been returned from a Sydney museum vault. They were not buried in the 'white' Pioneer cemetery.

In cemeteries, racial groups show the negotiation of different meanings and powers in relationship to each other. The way cemeteries are arranged acts as a check to see if the cross-cultural applies to other social groups, and also to verify the validity as an ideological context (Hodder, 1986, p. 67). Bama cemeteries indicate territoriality through descent, indicating group membership. Like the Chinese, they like their loved ones to be safely buried above the high watermark.

CHAPTER 22
SECRETS IN THE STONE

Recent discoveries by archaeologists have shed new light on the Bama tools. Stone axe heads and the flakes struck off stone cores for halfted spears have been found at Gwalapuram in southern India, above and below the volcanic ash which exploded out of Toba in Sumatra about 74,000 years ago.

The huge ash fallout was devastating but the humans adjusted to their new environment and carried on their craft, says Chris Clarkson, an archaeologist from the University of Queensland. From 80,000 years ago they began to make better use of the stone by knapping with multiple flakes off the core.

> 'By comparing the patterning, the Indian cores most resembled those made by modern humans in south Africa, southeast Asia and Australia. Tool-making is a skill and it takes a close apprenticeship to learn these methods, passed down the generations' (Clarkson quoted in Ravilious, 2010, pp 31-33).

However, stone hearths and artefacts always provide the most common evidence for stability or change in resource use (Morwood, 1995, p. 747ff). These artefacts were curiosities in the 1950s, when culture-and-anthropology was a frontier sideline. The ingenious stone technology of Bama artefacts was described (and collected for a museum) by Douglas Seaton.

Douglas Seaton described the Djabugay men's making of a stone axe, a 'naamba':

'A water-worn slate or sandstone is selected, egg-shaped, about one-inch-thick and tapering towards the edges. The edge is pounded thin with a hammer-stone and a groove pecked around the back edge to house the halft [the connecting part of the handle]. The edge is ground sharp. In some parts the back edge of the head is grooved and the halft fitted. A steel axe is called Na-kail, (ironstone).'

'The rainforest people use lawyer cane for the halft. Forest people use a handy sapling, sometimes they use a pair of straight-growing shoots, with the axe head tied in between them so that the shoots grew round it, the handle being cut off about fifteen inches along the halft. Green-skinned lawyer cane bound the head intricately and it was gummed in securely. This craft had been taught to Gwoyken, an initiated Djabugay, by his grandfather, and at first he was reluctant to produce on demand, but on payment of rations he was pleased to be able to show other Bama the skill to be remembered.

'On the way through the scrub Gwoyken began to forget his mission schooling and to use his Djabugay names for food and medicinal plants; he smelt a brown snake. Shortly after, he stood on a snake with his bare feet and leapt up in alarm. Seaton killed the snake. After this two older ladies came with two digging sticks, 'gunda', they had made and gave him, wanting rations in exchange. He was still a 'meecoola', Djabugay for someone not speaking the tribal tongue. Then they all returned home content as Boongua, the sun, went to camp behind the Boonda, the hills' (Seaton, 1959, p. 5).

Steven Fagan and Phillip Oui found one of these stone axe heads on the Fagan's property at Oak Forest, Kuranda, when the lawn was mown in 1995. The waisted flint tool was eight by thirteen centimetres; it was lying near two stone artefacts. He found a second axe head on the bank one metre outside the fence: it was revealed when the clay was washed away by heavy rain. It is eleven by seventeen centimetres, flat and quite sharp. Also called a 'tommyhawk' and 'narkile' by them, the axe was used by the Bama men to hammer, chop meat and plants and as a weapon.

Similar ground-edge stone axes have been found at Widgengarri in the West Kimberley dated at 28,000 years, at Nombe in Papua New Guinea and dated at 25,000 years (Holdaway, 1995, p. 790), and at Mackay to the south of Kuranda. An axe at Sandy Cape on Cape York is from before the last glacial maximum.

On the Fagans' property a nut-cracking stone, a 'walba', with thirteen grinding pits, was also found amongst the grass. It was used for cracking grey nuts, walnuts ('djanda'), cycad nuts ('gurnda') and black pine nuts. Some pits also contained red ochre ground into the sandstone. The area on the property is a habitation clearing in the rainforest about thirteen kilometres from Kuranda, with a nearby clear stream. From this place the Bama made regular foraging and trading expeditions up to seventeen kilometres away. The 'holiday camp' near the Barron River was 800 metres away. After the Bama moved to the mission, a post office was built on the home site; later it became a dwelling (Fagan and Oui, 1994).

Pam Oui demonstrates stone axes, Cairns, 1996

CHAPTER 23

BUSH FOODS AND TOOLS

The Bama roamed the coastal plains and tablelands less and less as other populations arrived to occupy those hunting lands. The rainforest slopes were their refuge; they camped near clear water and food trees, especially in the Wet.

The first Australians made economical wood and stone tools. They would make fibres by rolling threads on their thighs, using their toes and teeth for tensioning; everything was light and portable. They left to their descendants what they inherited from their ancestors. There were no native animals to be domesticated for plough or cart harness, so there was no point in making a wheel. There was no need for a pottery wheel for pots, which are too heavy for takeaway foods. There was no big bamboo for making knives or sea-going rafts then, when they arrived on the continent. Wide-angle boomerangs for open-plains hunting were not made in the rainforests.

Over generations, the Bama had worked out how to leach the toxins from seeds and nuts. The plants' alkaloids have an unpleasant smell and bitter taste which would have alerted the consumers to the presence of dangers. The toxin cycasin causes severe sickness and diarrhoea. The Bama removed it by dangling the pounded nuts in baskets of lawyer cane in the stream for some days. The fermented pulp was made into bread. 'Ricket nut' is another name for the large nuts from cycads (see Appendix 3).

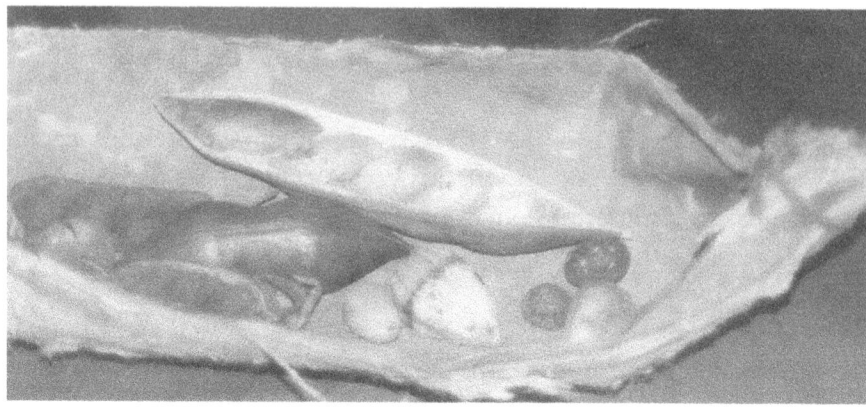

A bark coolamon displaying seeds such as black bean, cycad and yellow walnut at Tjapukai Aboriginal Cultural Park, Caravonica

The 'ooyurka' is a unique T-shaped slate tool with a short handle, altogether between fifteen and thirty centimetres long. It was used in the seed and nut grinding industry which was a specialty of the tribes who lived on the Tully and Johnstone Rivers. It is believed they used the grinding stone by rubbing it over a slab of slate incised with grooves. They ground the nuts and seeds between the stones to make a kind of flour. An example has been given to the convent museum at Cooktown.

Dr Richard Cosgrove has found stone implements up to 10,000 years old in the Innisfail area. With the approval of the Jirribal community, his archaeology team excavated a grinding industry site when the water levels were lowered in the Koombaloomba Dam on the Tully River, at Urumbal pocket. Round yellow walnut shells have been carbon dated at 5000 years old, or more.

The processed nuts and seeds can reveal their age because they have been heated, which firmly fixes the time when their tiny particles began to decay. As an example of the cooking, black bean seeds were roasted in the ground for twelve hours. They were then grated using snail shell and leached in running water in a dilly bag (Cosgrove, 2002, p. 7, 10).

Ground and leached seeds and nuts are also late Dry sea-

A nut-grinding stone

son staple foods. They were needed when the plains country, with its game reserves, was later taken over by other tribes. The importance of nuts to the Bama was especially clear during World War II. At the hospital at Jungarra, near the Kuranda railway Second Tunnel camp site (Mungarey), they made 'breast milk' from the nuts for mothers and babies.

The yellow walnut *Beilschmiedia Serrulatum*, and *Bancroftii* is a food tree. Its seeds need leaching, but they can be stored in ground pits for lean times, especially in the Wet. Though not prized as a cabinet timber, the soft wood can be easily made, with a stone axe, into a coolamon for carrying things. The wood is flattened by steam over a slow fire. The wood resists the ravages of decay when stored away and not exposed to air. Various tree barks are put to many uses—roofs, shelters, water and food containers, baby rests, paint boards and brushes.

Many of Far North Queensland's plants and nuts are also found in New Guinea, like the poisonous nut tree *Barringtonia racemosa*, which was used as both a food and a fish poison. The Cape York variety of *Terminalia melanocarpa*, the nut bean tree, is related to other varieties in Asia and the islands. *Canarium* is a gathered nut with related wild species in New Caledonia (Yen, 1995, p. 841). The yam, a staple food, came from Asia across the Wallace Line via New Guinea. There was one wild variety of rice, *Oryza rufopogon*, in swampy areas of the Barron River and Freshwater Creek.

Resins for glues, paints and waterproofing were found in the sap and seeds of vegetation. Chemicals were extracted from roots, seeds and leaves for medicines, for stunning fish, and for insect repellents. The Bama also made medicine for their people at Crystal Cascades, the sacred traditional area on Freshwater Creek. One was 'Milibun', their name for a sedative herb like valium.

Mona Fagan explained that the sap of the conjevoi lily stems was put on the poisonous hairs of the stinging tree to be scraped off when dry. Also called 'gympie gympie', this stinging tree's toxin will sting the skin severely in cold water for two months.

CHAPTER 24
CHANGING LAND AND SEAS

The aerial view of the North Queensland coastline is indeed fit for angels and ancestors, sweeping as it does from rainforest mountains to the aquamarine coral lagoons and reefs then the deep sea blue of straits and ancient river beds.

Tribal memories and the rich red schist of the soil attest to the volcanic activity of the ancient land. Damarri had an Inside Story for the Red Bluff of the Kuranda Range and for the big lakes on the Atherton Tablelands. Lake Eacham and Lake Barrine are in extinct craters. As well, Mt Hypipamee and Walsh's Pyramid are extinct craters dated at not less than 13,000 years ago (Dixon, 1991, p. 41). An Aboriginal myth tells how the Pyramid brought fire to the earth and how volcanic sparks formed the Milky Way. A Murri of the central Tully River had his own dramatic volcano story of the days of the ancestors when fire and flames suddenly shot up from the mountain and stones rained down; seen as an avenging evil spirit (Mjoberg, 1918/1986, p. 202).

At the Undara Volcanic National Park, 270 kilometres west of Cairns, the world's largest single lava tube system winds for sixty kilometres. The underground tunnel was formed by the cooling flow of magma and is dated at about 190,000 years ago. The underground caverns were believed to belong to the spirit people. The walls became too wet for painting with rock art.

A deep blue undersea gorge cuts through the outer barrier reef. The reefs nestle on the valleys lying under and beyond the sheltered waterways of the Whitsunday Islands. The picturesque peaks of the islands are the remains of a great volcanic crater which exploded about 100,000 years ago.

The islands were inhabited by the Sea People, Aboriginal people with canoes, who also lived on the mainland. The Ngaro tribe operated from Nara Inlet on Hook Island with its sheltered bay, marine food supplies and a cave shelter which still displays their rock paintings, dated at 2,500 years old. 'Wirraba' was their name for South Molle Island, meaning 'stone axe'.

Juan knives are hand sized pieces of black glossy stone, sturdy enough for butchering fish, dugong, sea turtles and even small whales. By 3,500 years Before Present (BP), the Ngaro had become specialists in these stone tools for trading (Brampton, 1999, p. 4 and O'Connor and Veth, 2000). From the work of Bryce Barker, Lara Lamb and others, we know that axes, Juan knives and spear heads dated at 6,620 BP were made from the quarried siliceous tuff of the hillside.

Knives at the quarry dated at 9,000 BP were fashioned at a time when the sea level was rising. Kangaroo bones at camp sites reveal other prey caught by the Ngaro in days before inundation, over the hills and valleys now flooded. Environmental changes pressed on the Ngaro who remembered them until they were annihilated in the late nineteenth century.

Along with the volcanic islands, our reefs make up the unique Great Barrier museum of the world's corals, sea creatures, perhaps thousands of shipwrecks and maritime history. Settlements and tool making sites can be identified on islands in the reef.

Changing land and seas

Around the world, the climate got hotter and wetter from 9,000 years ago when the Pleistocene era changed to the (recent) Holocene, settling down about 8,000 years ago. Before this, Australia was larger and joined to New Guinea. The continent, we now call 'Sahul', had lowered sea levels and a big savannah woodland that obstructed the spread of swamp and rainforest plant species and some animals, like the cuscus. Several species of kangaroo thrived that are now extinct. The cassowary, birds of paradise and many other beautiful birds were common on this Sahul land.

The earliest human rainforest occupation date of 35,000 years is now from Yombon, New Britain (Pavlides and Gosden, 1994). This is a much earlier date than places in South East Asia, where 'Sunda' was drowned at the end of the Ice Age. This date strongly suggests that the north east Queensland rainforest culture has its original links with Melanesia. This idea is supported by the evidence that humans have successfully exploited and manipulated the Australian tropical rainforest since ancient times, more than 5,000 years ago. It was probably before the drowning of the Torres Strait land bridge that ran between New Guinea and Australia (Cosgrove, 1996, pp. 900–912). While the land bridge existed the Gulf of Carpentaria was just a lake 500 kilometres long and 250 kilometres wide (Thorne, 1989).

An example of the link between the Queensland rainforest and Melanesia can be seen in a story that Koiki Mabo told. He spoke about the way the Murray Island fishermen traditionally travelled in eighty-foot-long double outrigger canoes down to the coast near Rockhampton.

Dr Peter Kershaw has studied pollen and tiny grains of charcoal in a microscope. He has found a very ancient date for the fossil pollen and charcoal fragments in the drill core of the seabed.

He says this is where the first colonisers walked, made fires, hunted, canoed and fished (Kershaw, 1995, p. 656–673). These grains were deposited by the huge wash of the delta of the Barron River.

> The offshore coastal shelf is 40-80km wide....The offshore drilling platform site...8km east of the nearest reef and 45 km from the shoreline... indicates a long step-wise reduction from 140,000 BP with no clear human connection. However, a further forest decline around 45,000 BP is likely, at least partially, the result of human burning (Kershaw, 2000, pp.155-156).

Damarri is the ancestor figure occurring again in the vast theatre of Storywaters. Wherever there was a problem he was on hand. The waters were rising about the Green Island coast. He was out on the coastal reefs in a canoe with two wives when the sea began to rise and flood the whole land. Where the sun set, he could see the mountains and the red bluff high above the mainland coast. He paddled the canoe back and made for the mountain tops to escape the ocean. His wives could not swim fast enough and were drowned (Martyn, 1993, p. 9).

Mountains were also used to hide in or to escape from the hot Wet season. The occupation dates between 31,000 and 2,000 years ago in cave shelters in south east Cape York coincides with the rise in sea level as the Ice Age receded. The incoming sea reduced the good coastal plain hunting sites where there were fewer mosquitoes (David, 1993, p. 50–54).

When the sea was at its highest level after the Ice Age, on the mainland there were middens and beaches where there are now thriving suburbs, but it got cold again. This can happen when a large volcanic eruption occurs. Its fallout of smoke and ash creates icy winters. These events are dated between 12,000 and 6,000 years ago by the Ocean Drilling Platform out from Cairns, on the margins of the river and reef which are now further out in the sea. There was a fall in sea level of six metres between 8,400 and 8,000 years ago (Oppenheimer, 1998, p. 36).

Think palaeoshorelines to grasp this great 'underwater story'. Walk to Green Island from the mountains. Get wet. You would drift down or dive one hundred metres through the clear blue sea, to a long wide coral strand, 225 kilometres north east of Townsville. Then fifty metres below the ocean surface on the sea bed you would see the wedges of mangroves and mud, a sign that the shoreline had been rising. Perhaps there are middens and stone tools which have been covered with sand. As we compare early charts of depths and geology with recent ones we can plot the past.

The warming climate after the Ice Age caused three great floods around the world and dramatic changes in sea level were recorded in the Great Barrier Reef between 8,400 and 7,800 years ago, big rises and falls. Over 4,000 years the sea level rose by twelve metres from seventeen metres to five metres below today's level, with a surge of three centimetres a year at one time (Oppenheimer, 1998, p. 36). This was followed by a swampy period, the time of the mangroves, which saw an increase in the spread of crocodiles.

The islands of the Torres Strait were also formed. In recent times in the Strait the land stations of the pearling industry have marked its archaeological outline. This outline is being lost rapidly to new building. When the gold and silver-lip pearl beds were discovered around Warrior Island in 1869, a rush of divers came from many countries to turn the pearls into buttons and decorations. By 1886 over two hundred pearling sites had been established.

The Japanese presence is evident in the ruins of dwellings and stonework in graves, paths, walls and jetties on Wai Weer Island. Remains of the quarantine stations, leper lazarets, early fortifications and government outposts also have been documented (McPhee, 2001).

On Australia's north east maritime frontier lie traces of the many seafarers who rest below its waters. They dared the tides, winds and currents. To stand on the hill on Possession Island overlooking the Torres Strait, with the silvery sea around the giant jetty (which is Cape York) is to be at one with them, to find yourself so that you will never be small in spirit again. You will be facing the world, self-possessed.

A Green Island reef at low tide before the observatory was built.

CHAPTER 25
CONCLUSION

'Black and white histories are not innocent; they can be reconstructed and deconstructed from a framework of race and culture predating the Native Titles Act to identify what space Aborigines should occupy. We need to acknowledge the indigenous contribution to the national myth through its symbolism, while our "European" narrative reconstruction of the nation is crucial in reconciliation debates on republican committees and our belief in a sacred symbolic document, the constitution…Even though we may resist the loss of our innocence about our history, we add to the national myth of our rules and morals constantly through its symbols and icons. Try as we might to suppress them they keep thrusting forward into our ceremonies, such as the Aborigines dancing and the convict-striped shirts. On occasions the people refuse to suppress their delight in acknowledging a rebellious past' (Morton, 1993).

The British historian, Dr Arnold Toynbee and his wife were drawn to Australia to follow their lifelong dream to see our fabled distant land described by James Cook and Thomas Huxley and his grandson the biologist, Julian Huxley. I interviewed Professor Toynbee on the Green Island ferry in 1955. He was concerned about the collapse of civilisations, and he thought that making a happy universe out of the rainforest was a commendable achievement for the Aboriginal people. With limited resources and technology they showed what could be done.

Many years later, I was on the ferry at the quay in Rhodes, Greece, when I was returning to Turkey. An English woman boarded the ferry wearing a lovely T-shirt with Aboriginal motifs and 'Kuranda Rainforest' printed on it. Without a word I at once revealed my own T-shirt printed in tropical fish. 'Cairns' it read. We laughed.

Ready or not, Queensland is exhibiting how the reconciliation game is being played; we star in a drama in a tropical movie-setting. The hit-and-miss relationship of the between is part of the national culture in which we live. Sharing power may be a much larger step for the Gadja than they believe, easier said than done.

T-shirt talk is not enough.

Murris' past and the stories are theirs, with careful songs of ownership. However, we the citizens cannot any longer remain silent on the issues of our day. *Go boldly*. What is needed now is a world with dignity, justice and pride in which each of us has a place, secure enough while we are seeking our bright uplands. We can be unafraid to look at ourselves, scars, warts and all with dignity and pride. As we stand on the front verandah of our nation we will know who we are.

REFERENCES

Allen, Jim. 'When did humans first colonise Australia?', *Search*. vol. 20, no. 5, 1989.

Allen, Jim. 'Who owns the past?', *Archaeology lecture*. La Trobe University, 1996.

Anderson, Chris. Personal comment to Patsy Coverdale. Adelaide: 2001.

Attenborough, Sir David. *The Lost Gods of Easter Island*. ABC TV, 27 July 2003.

Birdsell, Joseph. *Micro-evolutionary patterns in Aboriginal Australia: a gradient analysis of clines*. New York: Oxford University Press, 1993.

Bolton, Geoffrey. *Richard Daintree, a photographic memoir*. Brisbane: Jacaranda Press with Australian National University, 1969.

Bottoms, Timothy. *Djarrugan, the Last of the Nesting (M.A. Thesis)*. James Cook University, 1990.

Bottoms, Timothy. *The Bama—People of the Rainforest*. Cairns: Gadja Enterprises, 1992.

Bottoms, Timothy. *An Historical Overview of the Djabugay*. Cairns: NQ Research Associates, 1995.

Brampton, Margaret. 'Team unearths ancient aboriginal knives', *USQ News*. University of Southern Queensland, 16 June 1999.

Brayshaw, H. 'Ethnohistory and archaeology in the Herbert and Burdekin Rivers basin', *Lecture*. James Cook University, 1975.

Brook, Stephen. 'Study disputes snake evolution', *The Weekend Australian*. 5–6 February, 2000.

Bullen, M. *Signs of Women: a Study of paintings of women in rock art galleries of south east Cape York and Deaf Adder Creek*. La Trobe University, 1987.

Cannon, Michael. *Australia in the Victorian Age*, vol. 2. Melbourne: Thomas Nelson, 1973.

Carrick, Damien. *The Law Report*. ABC Radio National, 13 October 2009.

Clark, Gregory. 'Plenary Address', *Globalising Australia Conference*. La Trobe University, 20 July 1997.

Collinson, J. W. *Early Days in the North*. Brisbane: W R Smith and Paterson, 1939.

'The Commonwealth Housing Survey', *Statistical Geography, vol. 1 — Australian Standard Geographical Classification*, Australian Bureau of Statistics, July 2006.

Congdon, Brad. 'Interview by Robyn Williams', *The Science Show*. ABC Radio National, 8 August 2009.

Cosgrove, Richard. 'Origin and Development of Australian Aboriginal Tropical Rainforest Culture; a reconsideration', *Antiquity*, vol. 70, Edition 270, 1996.

Cosgrove, Richard. 'Forbidden fruit and how to eat them', *La Trobe University Bulletin*, March 2002.

Cowlishaw, Gillian. 'Lecture', *History Conference*. La Trobe University, 1992.

David, Bruno. 'Narrabulgin cave excavation', *Archaeology in Oceania*, vol. 28, no. 1, 1993.

David, Bruno et al. 'Glassy Obsidian artefacts from North Queensland: the Nolan's Creek source and some archaeological occurrences', *The Artefact*, vol. 15, 1992.

Dixon, R. M. W. *Words of our Country: Stories, Place Names and Vocabulary in Yidiny, the Aboriginal Language of the Cairns—Yarrabah Region*. University of Queensland Press, 1991.

Dodson, Mick. 'Speech', *Forum celebrating the Indigenous referendum*. Melbourne University, May 1997.

Dodson, Mick. 'Speech at Indigenous Leadership Centre, Coolangatta', *The Weekend Australian*, 26 October 2002.

Doran, Jenny. *Restructuring Awards: Issues for Women Workers*. Australian Council of Trade Unions, November, 1988.

References

Eades, Diana. *Aboriginal English and the Law: Communicating with Aboriginal English Speaking Clients: A Handbook for Legal Practitioners*. Brisbane: Queensland Law Society, 1992.

Eades, Diana. *Aboriginal English in the Courts: A Handbook*, Brisbane: Queensland Government.

Easdown, Geoff. 'Unravelling Spider's Web', *Townsville Bulletin* and *Herald Sun,* 20 July 2002.

Edwards, Ron. *Northern Folk*, no. 21, February 1968.

Edwards, Ron. *The Australian Yarn*. University of Queensland Press, 1996.

Fagan, Mona. Interview by Patsy Coverdale. 1996.

Fagan, Steven and Oui, Kylie. Oral history recorded for Patsy Coverdale. 2 October 1994.

Fawcett, Percy H. *Exploration Fawcett*, London: Hutchinson, 1953.

Fitzgerald, Ross et al. *Made in Queensland; a new history*. University of Queensland Press.

Garbarino, James et al. *Children in Danger: Coping with the consequences of community violence, Social and Behavioural Science series*. New York: Jossey-Bass, 1998.

Gilroy, Rex. *Australian Post*, 24 December, 1981.

Gonzales, Silvia. '2006 interview by Robyn Williams', *The Science Show*, ABC Radio National, 9 October 2010.

Goode, William J. *The Celebration of Heroes: prestige as a control system*. University of California Press, 1978.

Haebich, Anna. *Broken Circles—Fragmenting indigenous families 1800–2000*. Fremantle Arts Centre Press, 2000.

Hagenauer, F. A. 'Report to William Hodgkinson', *The Brisbane Courier,* 9 November 1886.

Harvey, David. *The Condition of Post-Modernity—An enquiry into the origin of cultural change*. Oxford: Basil Blackwell, 1989.

Hayes, Jacqui. 'Report', *The Science Show*. ABC Radio National, 9 October, 2010.

Hebdidge, Dick P. *Subculture: the meaning of style.* London: Methuen, 1979.

Hill, Kelvin. Interview by Patsy Coverdale, 1993.

Hodder, Ian. *Reading the Past.* Cambridge University Press, 1986.

Holdaway, Simon. 'Stone Artefacts and the Transition', *Antiquity* vol. 69, Edition 265, September 1995.

Hooper, Chloe. *The Tall Man: death and life on Palm Island*, Melbourne: Hamish Hamilton, 2008.

Horsfall, Nicky. *Living in Rainforest: the prehistoric occupation of North Queensland's humid tropics.* James Cook University, 1987.

Howe, Adrian. *Media and Violence Debate and Public Discourse Symposium.* University of Melbourne, 4 October 1996.

Hunter, Ernest. Quoted in *Bringing them home—National Enquiry into the Separation of Aboriginal and Torres Strait Islander Children from their families.* Human Rights and Equal Opportunity Commission, 1997.

Janke, Terri. *Butterfly Song.* Penguin, 2005.

Kamrin, Janice. *Ships from the Nile: The Cosmos of Khnumhotep and his partner Niankhkhum at Beni Hasan.* 1998.

Kershaw, A. Peter. 'Symposium on Archaeological Dating', *Archaeological and Anthropological Society of Victoria*. University of Melbourne, July 1993.

Kershaw, A. Peter. 'Environmental change in Greater Australia', *Antiquity* vol. 69, Edition 265, September 1995.

Kershaw, A. Peter and Patrick T. Moss. 'The last glacial cycle from the humid tropics of northeast Australia: comparison of a terrestrial and a marine record', *Palaeo*, vol. 155, 2000.

Kidd, Rosalind. *The Way We Civilise.* University of Queensland Press, 1997.

References

Nick, Kowalenko. Quoted in *Bringing them home—National Enquiry into the Separation of Aboriginal and Torres Strait Islander Children from their families.* Human Rights and Equal Opportunity Commission, 1997.

Law, Benjamin. 'Nowhere Land', *The Big Issue Australia,* edition 329, June 2009.

Edmund, Leach. *Culture and Communication: the logic by which symbols are connected.* Cambridge University Press, 1976.

Loney, Jack. *Wrecks on the Queensland Coast: 1791–1992.* Yarram: Oceans Enterprises, 1993.

Loos, Noel. *Invasion and Resistance: Aboriginal—European relations on the North Queensland Frontier 1861–1897.* Australian National University Press, 1982.

Low, Tim. *The New Nature: winners and losers in wild Australia.* Viking Penguin, 2002.

Lumholtz, Carl. *Among Cannibals.* Oslo: 1888.

Lynn, Robyn et al. *Murri Way: Aborigines and Torres Strait Islanders reconstruct social welfare practice.* Centre for Social Research, James Cook University, 1998.

Mabo, Bonita. Quoted on *Every Day Brave.* SBS TV, 18 October 2002.

Mackenzie, Geraldine. *Aurukun Diary: Forty years with the Aborigines.* Melbourne: The Aldersgate Press, 1981.

Martin, Alec. *Passages of Time: A Guide to the History of Far North Queensland,* vol. 2. The Cairns Post, 1990s.

Martyn, Julie. *The History of Green Island—the place of spirits.* Julie Martin, 1993.

Mathews, Colin. Interview by Patsy Coverdale, 2009.

McAllister, Peter. *Pygmonia: My Quest for the Secret Land of the Pygmies.* University of Queensland Press, 2010.

McBryde, Isabel. 'A Once and Future Archaeology', *Archaeology in Oceania,* vol. 21, no. 1, April 1986.

McHugh, Evan. *Shipwrecks: Australia's Greatest Maritime Disasters*. Viking Penguin, 2003.

McKnight, David. *From Drinking to Hunting*. Abingdon: Routledge, 2002.

McPhee, Ewen. 'Archaeology in the Torres Strait', *Marine Archaeology Conference*. Geelong, 2001.

Menzies, Gavin. *1421—The Year China Discovered the World*. London: Bantam Press, 2002.

Miller, David and Christopher Tilley. *Ideology, Power and Prehistory*. Cambridge University Press, 1984.

Mincham, Hans et al. *Incredible Australia*. Melbourne: Budget Books, 1978.

Mjoberg, Eric. *Amongst the Stone Age People in the Queensland Wilderness*, translated into English by S.M. Fryer. Brisbane: Oxley Library, 1986.

Moore, David and Rodney Hall. 'Boy's image no. LTF994M78A', *Australia, Image of a Nation 1850–1950*. Sydney: Collins, 1983.

Moore, Thomas. *The Re-enchantment of Everyday Life*. Hodder Headline, 1996.

Morwood, M. J. and D. R. Hobbs. 'Themes in the prehistory of tropical Australia', *Antiquity* vol. 69, Edition 265, 1995.

Morton, John. 'Singing Subjects and Sacred Objects', *Oceania*, vol. 15, 1987.

Morton, John. 'Mabo', *Aborigines and Australia Conference*. La Trobe University, 1993.

Mudrooroo. *Us Mob*. HarperCollins, 1996.

Mudrooroo. Interview. ABC Radio National, 30 July 2009.

Neves, Walter and Michael Heckenburger. Quoted in *Lost worlds: Secret Cities of the Amazon*. SBS TV, 14 February 2010.

Oliver, W. S. *Moments in Time: History Collection of The Cairns Post*, The Cairns Post, 2002.

Oliver, W. S. *Sugar*, The Cairns Post.

References

Oliver, W. S. *The Mulgrave Central Mill: fifty years in retrospect 1895–1945*, The Cairns Post.

Oppenheimer, Stephen and P. Larcome. *Eden in the East: the drowned continent of South East Asia*, Phoenix Books, 1998.

Parkinson, Sydney. *A Journal of a Voyage to the South Seas in His Majesty's ship The Endeavour: faithfully transcribed from the papers of the late Sydney Parkinson.* London: C. Dilly, 1784. *Facsimile edition.* Dover, N.H., USA: Caliban Books, 1984.

Patz, Elizabeth. 'Djabugay', *The Handbook of Australian Languages: the Aboriginal Language of Melbourne and other grammatical sketches.* R.M.W. Dixon and Barry J. Blake (eds). Oxford University Press, 1991.

Pavlides, Christina and Chris Gosden. '35,000 year old sites in the rainforests of West New Britain, Papua New Guinea', *Antiquity*, vol. 68, edition 260, 1994.

Peterson, Nicholas. 'Man and Environment, a symposium paper', *Archaeological and Anthropological Society of Victoria.* Melbourne, 1993.

Pessis, Anne-Marie. Quoted on documentary. SBS TV, 25 December, 2000.

Pike, Glenville. *The Men Who Blazed the Track: Pathfinders of the Cairns Range Commemorated.* Mulgrave Shire Council, 1956.

Pride, Patsy. 'Caught in flood', Brisbane: *The Courier-Mail*, 1948.

Raphael, Beverley. *Mental health report.* Victorian Government, 1996.

Ravilious, Kate. 'Exodus on the exploding earth', *New Scientist*, 17 April 2010.

Reynolds, Henry. *The Other Side of the Frontier: Aboriginal resistance to the European invasion of Australia.* Penguin, 1982.

Reynolds, Henry. *Aboriginal Sovereignty.* Allen and Unwin, 1996.

Ring, Ian. 'Wanted: a proper treaty and humane policy', *The Australian* newspaper, 30 April 2001.

Roughsey, Dick. *Moon and Rainbow.* Sydney: A. H. and A. W. Reed, 1971.

Rudd, Kevin. Quoted at a meeting of the Council of Australian Governments, as reported on ABC TV *News*, 7.00 pm, 2 July 2009.

Scanlon, John and Michael Lee. 'Wonambi Barriei', *Nature*, 5 February, 2000.

Skeene, George. *Two cultures: children from the Aboriginal camps and reserves in Cairns City: an autobiography: the life of George Skeene*. Kuranda: The Rams Skull Press.

Scott, Leisa. 'Dark Secrets, White Lies', *The Australian* magazine, 2 March 2002.

Scott, Leisa. 'Black Baby Deaths Don't Figure', *The Weekend Australian*, 29 June 2002.

Seaton, Douglas. 'Making a stone axe (naamba) in North Queensland', *North Queensland Naturalist*, no. 22, 31 March, 1959.

Smith, Bernard. *Imagining the Pacific: in the wake of the Cook voyages*, Melbourne University Press, 1992.

Smith, R. ABC Television, 10:55pm, 13 May 2001.

'Captive Lives', *South Australian Museum Newsletter*. South Australian Museum, February 1999.

Staff, Ian A. and Charmian P. Ahern. 'Symbiosis in Cycads with special reference to *Macrozamia communis* by D. W. Stevenson and K. J. Norstog (eds); The biology, structure and systematics of the Cycadales'. *Proceedings: Cycad 90, the second international conference on cycad biology*, Palm and Cycad Societies of Australia, 1993.

Stevens, Henry N. (eds.) *New Light on the discovery of Australia as revealed by the journal of Capt. Don Diego de Prado y Tovar, translated by George F. Barwick*. London: Henry Steven, Son and Stiles, 1919.

Sutton, Peter. 'Last Chance Operations in Far North Queensland in 1970's', *The Language Game: papers in memory of Donald C. Laycock*, T. Dutton, M. Ross and D. Tryon (eds). Australian National University, 1992.

Sutton, Peter. ABC Television, 2 July 2009.

Thompson, Donald. *Kinship and Behaviour in North Queensland: a preliminary account of kinship and social organization on Cape York Peninsula*, H. W. Scheffer (ed.), no. 51, series no. 7. Australian Institute of Aboriginal Studies, 1972.

Thorne, Alan G. *Man on the Rim: the peopling of the Pacific*. Angus and Robertson, 1989.

Thorne, Alan G. 'Lecture', *Australian Historical Biography Association Conference*. Melbourne, 1995.

Trahair, Richard. *Sociology Lecture in Psychopolitics*, La Trobe University, September, 1991.

Trudgen, Richard. *Why Warriors Lie Down and Die*. Darwin: Aboriginal Resources and Development Services Inc., 2000.

Unaipon, David. *Legendary Tales of the Australian Aborigines*. Melbourne: Miegunyah, 2001.

Valley Weekly, Melbourne. 15 June, 2005.

West, Japananka Errol. *Lecture at the Referendum forum*, Government Aboriginal Education Policy Unit, Southern Cross University, 1997.

Wolf, Naomi. *The Beauty Myth: how images of beauty are used against women*. New York: William Morrow and Co., 1991.

Wood, G. Arnold. *The Voyage of the Endeavour*. South Melbourne: Macmillan, 1970.

Yen, D. E. 'The development of Sahul agriculture with Australia as bystander, *Antiquity* vol. 69, Edition 265, September 1995.

Yu, Peter. Quoted on *Four Corners*. ABC Television, 3 September 2001.

APPENDIX 1

J. Birdsell on the Bama survey

A ground-breaking survey of the Bama in the North Queensland rainforest was undertaken during 1938 and 1939 by anthropologists, Dr Joseph Birdsell and Dr Norman Tindale. The study detailed names and lineage by recording their details and taking photographs of the people. Today these photographs are invaluable for family identification and genealogy.

Dr Birdsell's database, which was fully analysed again in 1993, included information about ninety-five full-blooded Aboriginal people, largely Djabugay, of the Kuranda region. It included thirty-one adult males, twenty-six adult females, twenty boys and eighteen girls:

> 'The Kongkandji [Gungganydji] in the group showed a frequency of 0.98 of the gene, their neighbors the Idindji [Yidiny] a value of 0.90 and slightly further inland adjoining people, the Tjapukai [Djabugay] have a frequency of 0.83. The validity of this clinal trend seems justified, even if samples are small. This area of high values presumably represents a residue involving early waves of incoming peoples, the ancestors of the present day Barrineans. Values for the N gene are very high in New Guinea and, significantly, gene frequencies are considerably lower in Upper Cape York next to New Guinea. The rain forest is a special environment and all evidence points to its having been a refuge area for many millennia.'
> (Birdsell, 1993, p. 36)

Dr Birdsell's research shows that surprisingly large differences in gene frequencies can occur between adjacent and inter-

Appendices

marrying tribal groups. Gene frequencies are not simple and not direct measures of relationship between populations. This is the nature of microevolution.

Mincham et al., (1978, p.188) has a photograph of Dr Birdsell making his study of the Queensland Aboriginal people.

APPENDIX 2

F. A. Hagenauer on Wujal Wujal

The inner geography of myth grows out of the stories like the following one of country which is now in the area of Wujal Wujal, on the coast north of Cape Tribulation.

Aboriginal tribes share artefacts and culture between the Herbert River area and the Bloomfield River. They were visited in 1885 by a Moravian missionary, Reverend F. A. Hagenauer, who went to Victoria from the Missionary College at Ebersdorff (Germany) in May 1858. He was sent on a holiday to North Queensland due to overwork at the mission he had established at Ramahyuck in Gippsland, after considerable obstruction by pastoralists. He surveyed the Cairns area of the coast but did not want to be the occupants' first taste of Christianity. He established a mission at Mappoon on Cape York Peninsula, which was given a church bell in his memory.

William Hodgkinson received the following report describing Hagenauer's northern visit, published in *The Brisbane Courier*, on 9 November, 1886. It is held at the Melbourne Museum.

'Perhaps it is just as well to state here that a few days later we were accompanied in the large boat belonging to the Vilele estate by some young gentlemen from the plantations of Messrs Hislop and Co. to the first great waterfall of the Bloomfield about six or eight miles up the river from the entrance into Weary Bay. The river is from 300 to 400 feet wide and in some places very deep. The banks on both sides are a continuation of mountains rising at some places very high and reach at a distance [Mt Peter Botte] the height of 3,300 feet. The most charming aspects meet the eye every turn of the river, for the whole ground up to the mountain tops is covered with the most beautiful tropical trees, shrubs, and creepers, many of them in full bloom.

'The river seems well supplied with fish, but the horrible alligator has his habitation there also, and is really a terror to man and beast. Not long ago Mr F. Bauer shot a large one dead, through the eye, which seems the only spot where a ball can enter. Strange to say, the great animal had in the other eye two sharp spear ends from the weapons of the Aboriginals, thereby showing that the brute had been hunted before. We saw the heavy skin or hide, likely to be made ready for some exhibition or museum, in a city of the south. The flesh gave a kind of alligator banquet to the Aborigines, who enjoyed it very much, for they seem to take great pleasure in feasting upon the bodies of their enemies.

'At one very gloomy looking spot several miles up the river, under the overhanging trees, is a great stone, on and under which a great evil spirit dwells, according to the statements of the blacks, who are so much frightened that they will not pass the locality, and if it happens that any of them are in the large boat belonging to the plantation, they will stoop down and hide themselves, so that the evil spirit cannot see nor catch them. I have an idea that once upon a time one of these alligator monsters had taken down and devoured one of the Aboriginals near this great stone. The place looks very much like one where this would occur, and when we touched the stone and looked into the clear, green, deep water we naturally did so with great care and caution ... Hagenauer (1886)'

APPENDIX 3

T. Bottoms, I. A. Staff and C. P. Ahern on plant toxins

'In potential toxic seeds, the poisons enabled them to keep stored in earth pits for famines or ceremonial gatherings, but the slow release toxins, if not fully soaked out in water, are now known to affect brain tissue seriously up to 25 years later. It is hard for traditional staple foods, even, cassava, to be seen as lethal substances by folk dependent on them; this is common throughout the Pacific region. They are part of the rhythm of life, as when the Bama saw that the stemshoot of the cycas media stood erect then rain would come; it was humidity sensitive' (Bottoms, 1990, p. 61).

The human gut has no enzymes to digest fructans polymers, but the fatty acids slow digestion down to reduce the rapid rise of blood glucose that produces diabetes. Cyanobacteria, blue-green algae, are essential for protein manufacture through nitrogen fixing in the cycad, macrozamia. This is essential for making plant protein, especially at times of heavy rain (Staff and Ahern, 1993, pp. 200–210).

APPENDIX 4

E. Mjoberg on cannibals

The Chinese were particularly hated by Aborigines, who killed innumerable Chinese goldminers.

'Old goldminers who were at the Palmer rush told me that it was by no means uncommon to see roasted Chinese feet sticking out of the Aborigines' bags woven of rattan fibre, which they always take with them on journeys. A yellow life was not valued very highly in those days, so the whites usually let the black man go, as long as they did not attack and kill their comrades of their own white skin colour. In the end, the blacks developed a special taste for yellow men's flesh. They—[sic] themselves that it tasted much better than that of white men, because the flesh of Chinese was not as salt, but more like fish to taste. Probably this was due to the Chinamen's exclusive rice diet' (Mjoberg, 1918/1986).

APPENDIX 5

P. D. Coverdale on six fingers

A tribe of people from the Sepik River in Papua New Guinea traditionally saw people with six fingers as possessed of supernatural powers. This is one of the enduring common links in the great ancestral Oceanic worship of powerful sexdigital (six fingered) gods.

It was also the power of Make Make, the god of Easter Island, of Rapa Nui, where some of the stone statues had this magic. The great god's image was carved in wood. With its long hands, long gaunt body, large eyes and long ears it was housed there in its sacred cavern. The carving was given as a souvenir to a Tahitian, Mahine, and taken on board *HMS Resolution* in 1774 where it was painted by draftsman Roberts. His picture of Make Make was held at one time by the Museum of New South Wales at Sydney (Attenborough, 2003).

About the author

ABOUT THE AUTHOR

Patsy Coverdale grew up in 1950's Redlynch surrounded by the tropical rainforest and cane fields of North Queensland where she became the first qualified woman journalist at *The Cairns Post*.

She shared the lives, social changes and frontier history of both the black and white people around her.

Patsy learned from the University of Queensland and from visiting anthropologists and film makers from many parts of the world.

Patsy went to Britain in 1957, where she gained experience in journalism and public relations with Australia House. After tours of Britain and Europe, Patsy married Eric Coverdale and studied pottery, fossils and ancient settlements at Oxford until the birth of the first of their two sons.

In 1961, she returned with the family to Australia. Patsy visited the north regularly and, as both an Insider and an Outsider, discussed cultural and political events in the north with both Bama and white friends. She also gathered some stories of the coast, the hinterland and the reefs.

After an inspiring trip to Laura rock art and Lakefield National Park in 1990, she completed her Arts degree in Sociology at La Trobe University in 1994. Patsy wrote *North Queensland in Black and White* to show us culture, history and prehistory of the Bama people of the north and how far white settlers and the Bama have come to understand each other through years of blood, tears and triumph.

CATTAC PRESS

www.ingramcontent.com/pod-product-compliance
Ingram Content Group UK Ltd.
Pitfield, Milton Keynes, MK11 3LW, UK
UKHW021302180426
11947UKWH00015B/975